RETOLD TALES SERIES

RETOLD AMERICAN CLASSICS
 VOLUME 1

RETOLD AMERICAN CLASSICS
 VOLUME 2

RETOLD BRITISH CLASSICS

RETOLD WORLD CLASSICS

**RETOLD CLASSIC MYTHS
 VOLUME 1**

RETOLD CLASSIC MYTHS
 VOLUME 2

The Perfection Form Company, Logan, Iowa 51546

CONTRIBUTING
WRITERS

Michele Price
B.A. Communications
Educational Writer

William S. E. Coleman, Jr.
M.A.T. English and Education
Educational Writer

RETOLD TALES SERIES

RETOLD CLASSIC MYTHS

VOLUME 1

THE PERFECTION FORM COMPANY

Editor-in-Chief:
Kathleen Myers

Editors:
Beth Obermiller
Rebecca Spears Schwartz

Cover Art: Don Tate
Book Design: Dea Marks
Inside Illustration: Mark Marturello
                    Kevin Luttenegger

TABLE
OF CONTENTS

WELCOME TO THE RETOLD CLASSIC MYTHS

You see the references everywhere. Look at great artwork like the *Venus de Milo*. Or classic literature such as James Joyce's *Ulysses*. Then think about our language, which is filled with words like *typhoon* and *panic*. You can even see them in ads for FTD Florist and Atlas moving company.

What do all these things, from art to ads, have in common? They're based on Greek and Roman classic myths.

We call something classic when it is so well loved that it is saved and passed down to new generations. Classics have been around for a long time, but they're not dusty or out of date. That's because they are brought back to life by each new person who sees and enjoys them.

The *Retold Classic Myths* are stories written years ago that continue to entertain or influence today. The tales offer exciting plots, important themes, fascinating characters, and powerful language. They are stories that many people have loved to hear and share with one another.

RETOLD UPDATE

This book presents a collection of eight adapted classics. All the colorful, gripping, comic details of the older versions are here. But in the Retold versions of the stories, long sentences and paragraphs have been split up.

In addition, a word list has been added at the beginning of each story to make reading easier. Each word defined on that list is printed in dark type within the story. If you forget the meaning of a word while you're reading, just check the list to review the definition.

You'll also see footnotes at the bottom of some story pages. These notes identify people or places, explain ideas, show pronunciations, or even let you in on a joke.

We offer two other features you may wish to use. One is a two-part map of ancient Greece at the front of the book. The other is a list of the major gods, giving both their Greek and Roman names. You see, the Romans linked stories about their own gods to the Greek gods. So in many ways, the gods were identical. The list will help you keep all the names straight.

Finally, at the end of each tale you'll find some more information. These revealing and sometimes amusing facts will give you insight into ancient cultures, tellers of the myths, or related myths.

One last word. Since these myths have been retold so often, many versions exist. So a story you read here may differ from a version you read elsewhere.

Now on to the myths. Remember, when you read the Retold Tales, you bring each story back to life in today's world. We hope you'll discover why these tales have earned the right to be called classics.

MAPS OF ANCIENT GREECE

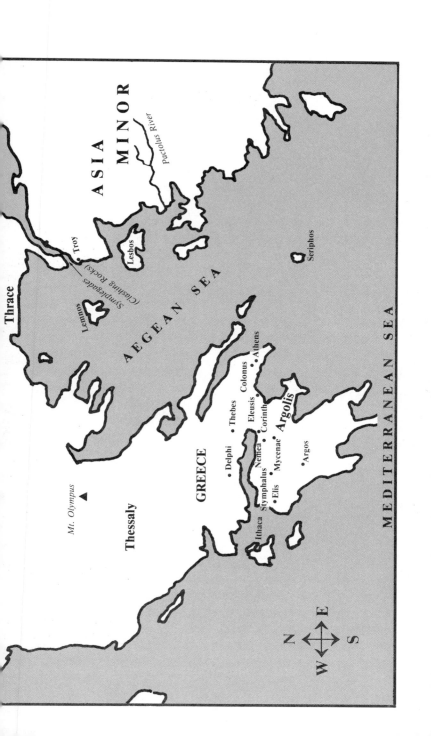

CREATION OF THE TITANS AND GODS

VOCABULARY PREVIEW

Below is a list of words that appear in the story. Read the list and get to know the words before you start the story.

agile—quick; nimble
compassion—mercy; kindness
counsel—advice
dethroned—removed from a throne; forced from power
eternally—through all ages; forever
guzzled—drank quickly or greedily
immortal—living forever; deathless
imprisoned—put into prison; jailed
inevitable—certain to happen; unavoidable
infinite—having no limits; endless
mocking—jeering; scornful
pelted—attacked; shelled or stoned
presented—gave
reign—period of rule
sickle—cutting tool with a curved blade
sprouted—grew
supreme—greatest; most powerful
thwarted—stopped; prevented
vial—small bottle
wretched—miserable; pitiful

CREATION
of the
TITANS and GODS

"With great power comes great fear."
Does that seem like a contradiction?
Not to the Greeks.
They wisely guessed that even
the mightiest ruler in the universe
would feel threatened.
So threatened, in fact, that he let his fear
swallow everything—
including his love.

In
the beginning was darkness.
Nothing existed.
No human form.
No plant, animal, or sea creature.
Not even the stars,
sound, or wind existed.
Just small bits of things floated
through **infinite** space. These things
were seeds for what would later
become everything that ever was.
These things and this space were called
Chaos.[1]

[1] (kā′ os)

After countless ages, the bits of things slowly began to swirl. They swirled faster and faster until the first **immortal** being, Eros[2]—or Love—appeared. Eros was the force of attraction that caused all other things to be.

Soon after, another immortal being was created. This was Erebus,[3] the black hole of death. His home was called Tartarus,[4] or the Underworld. Erebus then joined hands with his great sister, Night, and they wept. From their tears, Light and Day came into being.

Light and Eros danced on the spiral to create still another immortal being. She was Gaea,[5] the Earth. Her power was great and her belly brimmed with life.

Gaea gave birth to the Mountains and the Sea. But her belly wasn't empty yet. She next gave birth to the greatest of all her children: Uranus,[6] the Sky. Gaea made this son her equal so he would surround her on all sides.

Then Gaea produced the Stars and the Four Seasons. After the delivery of these children, she married her son Uranus. He then became the **supreme** ruler of all creation.

Gaea and Uranus had many children together. Their first three offspring were the Hundred-handed Ones. Each of these giants **sprouted** fifty heads from his mighty shoulders. And each had a hundred mighty arms swinging in all directions. They were named Cottus, the Furious; Briareus, the Vigorous; and Gyges, the Big-limbed.[7]

The next three children of Gaea and Uranus were the Cyclopes.[8] Each of these frightening creatures had one huge eye in the middle of his forehead. The mighty Cyclopes controlled the storm powers. Brontes was Thunder. Steropes was Lightning. And Arges was the Thunderbolt.[9]

Uranus looked upon his offspring with horror. He knew

[2] (er' os or ē' ros)
[3] (er' e bus)
[4] (tar' tar us)
[5] (jē' a or gē'a)
[6] (ū' ra nus or ū rā' nus)
[7] (kot' us) (brī ar' e us or brī ā' re us) (jī' jēz)
[8] (sī klō' pēz)
[9] (bron' tēz) (ster' ō pēz) (ar' jēz)

that their strength would be far greater than his own.

Uranus took care of this threat in a brutal way. After each son was born, Uranus hurled him deep into the earth.

For nine days and nine nights the sons fell before finally landing in Tartarus. There they were instantly chained to the floor, never to see light again. And what a **wretched** prison! Deep, dark Tartarus was as far below the earth as the stars are high above.

After each child was safely **imprisoned**, Uranus chuckled. He was now happy and content that his position as ruler would never be challenged. "I'll rule over earth and everything forever!"

Gaea, on the other hand, was shocked by her husband's actions. She deeply grieved for her children. Yet she kept her feelings quiet, for she knew revenge would be hers one day. She had the power of foreseeing the future.

The next children born to Gaea and Uranus were the thirteen nature gods, the Titans.[10] The Titans possessed the powers of earthquakes, volcanos, and hurricanes. Among them was Helios, god of the sun, and his sister Selene, goddess of the moon. Oceanus,[11] the god of the rivers which circled the globe, was a Titan as well. Others were Cronus, Rhea, Atlas, and Prometheus.[12]

With the birth of the Titans, Gaea realized the time had come to take revenge against Uranus. So she took a piece of stone and shaped it into a sharp **sickle**. Then she went to her sons.

"Your father is very cruel," she said in a voice that sounded like a huge whirlwind. "He imprisoned your brothers in Tartarus because he feared them. So now I need your help. We must defeat Uranus and rescue your brothers."

Her sons were silent. They were terrified of their father's power. How could they ever risk what their mother was suggesting?

[10](tī′ tanz)
[11](hē′ li os) (se lē′ nē) (ō sē′ a nus)
[12](krō′ nus) (rē′ a) (at′ las) (prō mē′ thūs or prō mē′ thē us)

A soft chuckle came from behind Gaea's sons. It came from the youngest son, Cronus. He was laughing at his cowardly brothers.

"Not one of you has the courage to help Mother? I'm surprised at you," Cronus said with a **mocking** smile.

He pushed his way past his tall brothers to the front. "Well, never leave to others what you can do yourself. Mother, I'll help you! I'm not afraid!"

Gaea gazed knowingly at her brave son. As she had foreseen, Cronus was the only one with enough daring to destroy Uranus.

Gaea **presented** the sharp sickle to Cronus. "Be careful with this blade, my son. Its sharp edge is for your father, not for you. Tonight, hide in the bushes by the sea. I will sleep there with Uranus. Your sister Selene will be there to help you as well."

That evening, they carried out their plan. After Helios had carried the sun across the sky and gone to sleep, Uranus came to the sea. He saw his wife by the shore and lay down next to her.

In the bushes nearby, Cronus crouched. The night was so black that he could barely make out his father's sleeping figure. He would have to wait for his sister to appear.

It wasn't long before Selene rose to shine the moon brightly over Uranus. Cronus could now easily see his father's figure. Quietly he crept out from his hiding place and over to Uranus' side. Then raising the sickle high in the air, he brought it down and wounded his father.

Cronus laughed and then shouted triumphantly. "Your time as ruler has ended, Father! No one will support you once they find out how weak you are. I now rule over all that exists! Challenge me if you dare, but you'll see I'm far greater! So be wise for once and accept your fate."

Of course, Uranus was immortal and could not die. But he could feel pain. And at the moment, knowing his **reign** was over pained him more deeply than his wounds.

Gaea now quickly turned to the new god of the sky. "Well done, my son. And now it's time to release your brothers from their dark prison."

Cronus stepped back with a cruel smile. "I didn't overthrow my father for you," he declared. "I did it for me. I'm now supreme ruler. That means even you must bow to my wishes! I have no reason to release my brothers except to please you. And that isn't enough."

Gaea knew that behind his bold words, Cronus was just like his father. He also feared the power of the Cyclopes and Hundred-handed Ones.

Gaea glared at her son. "Cronus, you may have won your father's throne. But believe me, it doesn't end here. You also will be **dethroned** by one of your sons. That is *your* fate."

Cronus laughed. "I'll fool fate just as I've fooled you! I will have no children. Therefore, I'll reign forever!"

At first, it seemed that Cronus would indeed triumph. But in time, fate began to work on him. He fell in love with and married his sister, Rhea. And soon she presented a beautiful baby girl to her husband.

Cronus gazed at little Hestia[13] with adoring eyes. Suddenly Gaea's words screamed in his head. Cronus' eyes became boiling pools of madness. He grabbed the baby from Rhea's arms and quickly swallowed her. "There!" he thought to himself. "The child is gone. Fate has been defeated."

Rhea had four more children: two daughters, Demeter and Hera, and two sons, Hades and Poseidon.[14] Each time Cronus demanded to see the infant. And each time, he madly seized the babe and swallowed it.

Rhea's heart cried with longing. She wanted children so much. Yet it was **inevitable** that her cruel husband would destroy every one.

Finally Rhea sought out her mother, Gaea. "Mother, I beg you for help," she said. "I am pregnant again. And

[13](hes' ti a)
[14](de mē' ter) (her' a or hē' ra) (hā' dēz) (pō sī' don)

even now Cronus is waiting, ready to swallow this poor babe, too. Please, I don't want him to take this one. What can I do?''

Gaea comforted her daughter. ''I understand the pain you feel, dear Rhea. Cronus is as heartless as his father. I will help you.''

Gaea drew a chair up for her daughter and then quietly spoke. ''When you are about to give birth, go to the isle of Crete,''[15] she said. ''You'll find a cave hidden on its northern slope. Have your baby there. The nymphs[16] will feed it goat's milk. And I will make sure Cronus does not hear its cries.''

''But what about Cronus?'' Rhea asked.

Gaea smiled. ''Clever Cronus. I know a trick to fool him. Since he expects you to give him the child, do so. But to a father with a heart of stone, why not present a stone? After you give birth, find a rock the size of a baby. Wrap that in a blanket and offer it to Cronus. He'll swallow it whole without ever suspecting.''

Rhea followed her mother's advice. She gave birth to a baby son, Zeus,[17] on the isle of Crete. Then she returned to her husband with the well-wrapped rock.

As soon as Cronus heard news of the birth, he came to Rhea's side. He bent down beside her and gazed sweetly upon the bundle in her arms.

For a moment, Rhea began to panic. The look on her husband's face was so loving. She feared Cronus might actually want this baby.

But as had happened five times before, Cronus' eyes grew mad. He seized the bundle, opened his huge mouth, and swallowed it. Then he smacked his lips happily.

''There!'' he thought once again. ''The child is gone. I have **thwarted** fate again. No one is cleverer than I am!''

[15](krēt)

[16](nimfs) Nymphs were a group of minor nature goddesses who lived in rivers and trees.

[17](zūs)

But Cronus wasn't quite as clever as he thought. For not only had he swallowed a rock. He also failed to realize that fate is never fooled.

Time passed and Zeus became a handsome young god. He was smart, loyal, and had a gentle heart. His grandmother helped see to that. Each day she taught him valuable lessons. He learned grace as well from dancing with the **agile** nymphs.

One day Gaea interrupted Zeus' play. With a sad and serious face, she told him about his past. She explained how and why his father, Cronus, had swallowed his brothers and sisters. She told him of his grandfather, Uranus, who had imprisoned her children. She also warned him about ruling with a selfish heart.

Finally she said, "Zeus, it is time for you to leave. You must go fulfill your fate." Then she handed him a small **vial**. "When your father is thirsty, give this to him to swallow. Don't fail us, Zeus."

Zeus nodded grimly and pocketed the vial. "I won't, Grandmother. I've learned well. You can be certain I won't follow in my father's footsteps."

Zeus went to his father's home. Quietly he let his mother know of his arrival. After their joyful reunion, Rhea and her son schemed together. "I will present you as a new cupbearer to Cronus," Rhea decided.

Rhea and Zeus carried out the plan without any trouble. Cronus gladly accepted the boy. He was pleased by the young, handsome Zeus.

Zeus' chance soon came. One day Cronus was very thirsty, so he called for Zeus. The young god was ready. He emptied the vial into Cronus' cup and brought it to his father.

Cronus **guzzled** every drop. He was about to ask for another cupful when he began to feel hot. A burning pain gnawed at his stomach.

Angrily, he accused Zeus. "Cupbearer! What did you serve me? I feel sick! Did you dare poison me?"

Suddenly Cronus vomited. The first thing that came out

of his mouth was the rock. Next came Zeus' two brothers, Poseidon and Hades. Then came his sisters, Hera, Demeter, and Hestia. Since they were gods, they were all alive and fully grown.

At that point, Rhea stepped into the room and stood next to Zeus. "Cronus, fate cannot be thwarted! It was said you would have a son who would overthrow you. Just as you overthrew your father! That son stands in front of you now. His name is Zeus."

Cronus bellowed, "Son or no son! No one will take my throne! He'll have to fight me and all the other Titans!"

Zeus accepted the challenge. With his brothers and sisters' aid, he declared war on Cronus and the Titans. But the two sides were too evenly matched. For ten long years the battle dragged on.

Finally the wisest of the Titans, Prometheus, went to Cronus. "I have a plan, Cronus," Prometheus said. "To win this battle, you need only free our brothers in Tartarus. With their strength, you could easily beat Zeus."

"I have no need for brothers!" Cronus angrily replied.

Prometheus realized Cronus was too stupid to accept the wise **counsel**. So he went to Zeus and gave him the same advice.

Zeus suddenly recalled Gaea's tale of her imprisoned children. He regretted not freeing them sooner.

Immediately Zeus and his brothers journeyed to the deep pit of the earth. There they killed the guard and freed the Cyclopes and Hundred-handed Ones. Then Zeus led them back to the light of earth.

Zeus gathered the gods and his uncles together. He feasted them on ambrosia and nectar, the food and drink of the gods. These precious foods give the gods immortality.

Then Zeus spoke. "We have been battling for ten years now. Uncles, I'm hoping you'll fight on our side. I wish to put an end to this long war."

Briareus answered his nephew. "And we wish to put an end to the Titans. We know how cruel they are. If you hadn't freed us, we would still be imprisoned forever in darkness. We'll help fight the Titans because we think you'll rule with greater wisdom and **compassion**."

Then the Cyclopes presented Zeus and his brothers with gifts. To Zeus, they gave the mighty thunderbolt. To Poseidon, they offered a three-pointed spear to create earthquakes and tidal waves. To Hades, they gave a cap which made him invisible. This, they told him, would help him sneak up on enemies.

Zeus and his brothers thanked the Cyclopes for the gifts. Then the young god stood and shouted, "Now let us rise and fight!"

With those words, a terrible battle began. The Hundred-handed Ones broke off huge boulders from cliffs. Then they **pelted** the Titans, causing the whole earth to shake. The shock waves reached as far as Tartarus.

From the heavens, Zeus flung bolts of thunder and lightning at Cronus. The fiery bolts caused the forests to catch fire. The seas boiled and bubbled, too. Even the sky hissed with flames and seemed ready to crash to the ground. The sound of fury and confusion was everywhere.

In the end, the gods conquered the Titans. The Hundred-handed Ones hurled Cronus and most of his fellow Titans into the pit of Tartarus. There they were chained. Two of the monsters offered to stay and guard them. Another one of the defeated Titans, Atlas, was forced to hold up the skies **eternally**.

Only one Titan escaped punishment: Prometheus. Because he had sided with Zeus, he was allowed his freedom.

Unlike his father and grandfather, Zeus wisely decided to share his power. Though he remained supreme ruler, he allowed others to control parts of his kingdom. To Poseidon, he gave the sea and to Hades, the Underworld. Zeus himself took control of the sky.

Finally a lasting peace had been found. The young gods climbed to the top of Mt. Olympus[18] to begin their reign.

[18] (ō lim′ pus)

INSIGHTS

Just what were the powers of the gods? They certainly had some magical powers. For instance, they could change shape, control nature, and travel somewhere in a moment. Many were wise and could even foretell the future. Plus they were often strong, forever young, and beautiful.

But there were exceptions to all these rules. None of the gods were all-knowing or all-powerful. In fact, a few were stupid and weak. And they all sometimes let anger, jealousy, or lust lead them into folly.

The gods also could be wounded and some could die. There were even ugly gods.

As you can see, the gods could be much like humans. Perhaps that is why stories about them have appealed to people for so long.

The Greeks called the shapeless, confused matter from which the universe was made *Chaos*. This word is used today to describe any situation which involves confused disorder.

In many mythologies, Heaven is located in some vague or general place. But the Greeks knew exactly where their gods lived. Mt. Olympus, located in northern Greece, is the country's highest mountain.

The name *Cronus* was probably a misspelling of the Greek word *chronos,* which means *time.* The same root word can be found in *chronological* (arranged according to time), *chronic* (lasting a long time), and *chronicle* (a record of events in the order they occurred).

Gaea, the goddess of the earth, was named for the Greek word meaning *earth.* Today we are reminded of her in such words as *geography* and *geology.* Even *geometry* comes from the same root since it means "the study of the measurement of the earth."

During the 1980s, a New Age philosophy developed that looked back to old age Greek philosophy. These Greek ideas cropped up again when some people suggested that the earth should be viewed as a living whole. Their name for this creature? Gaea!

PROMETHEUS

VOCABULARY PREVIEW

Below is a list of words that appear in the story. Read the list and get to know the words before you start the story.

awe—fear and wonder
coax—urge
commerce—trade; business
deceptive—misleading; false
defied—challenged or disobeyed
descent—a movement or journey downward
destined—certain; predecided
devour—gobble up; eat
fleets—groups (especially ships)
hovered—waited (especially at one place in the air)
humility—modesty; freedom from pride
provocation—cause or reason
rebellious—unwilling to obey
reliant—dependent
scavenge—search or dig for
soothed—calmed; comforted
stern—strict; harsh
tactic—plan; approach
tend—watch over; care for
unmercifully—without pity; cruelly

PROMETHEUS

*According to one Greek myth,
the early days of human life
were rough indeed. In those
days, the young race needed
plenty of help. But who would
dare offer aid when mighty
Zeus, the king of gods, forbid it?
In the end, only one brave god
stepped forward. But for that
courageous act, he paid a
great price.*

Prometheus followed the steep path to his favorite spot at the top of Mt. Olympus.[1] Then the Titan[2] carefully crawled out on a ledge and peeked over.

He couldn't see a thing. Sheets of rain pounded the earth below. Prometheus had felt almost certain they wouldn't be out on a day like this. Yet he wanted to make sure they were safe.

Prometheus pictured them crouched in their caves—cold, wet, and scared. They were probably hungry, too. He wanted to help them. He would do anything for them if he could. He loved those creatures—the creatures called humans.

[1](prō mē′ thūs or prō mē′ thē us) (ō lim′ pus)
[2](tī′ tan) As told in the previous story, Titans were one of the oldest races of gods. Most were imprisoned after losing a war against Zeus and his brothers and sisters. Prometheus was allowed to remain free because he aided Zeus.

Perhaps Prometheus loved the human race so much because he had created them. From a mix of earth and water, he had molded human shapes in the image of the gods. Then he blew the breath of life into those bodies. Finally he set humankind free to roam the earth.

But life on earth was not so easy for this new race. They were under the constant watch of Zeus,[3] the god of the sky.

Zeus was a great provider, but he was also a **stern** punisher. He gave humans wild beasts to eat. But he also threw mighty thunderbolts when he felt humans were acting too proud. If humankind didn't pray to Zeus and fear his power, he would destroy them.

Zeus also teased humans **unmercifully**. When he grew bored, he would sometimes amuse himself by scaring humans. He'd drop the biggest rainstorm he could gather. Or he'd split a few huge trees with lightning bolts.

Prometheus hated to see the young race forced to live under these conditions. He wanted them to be able to see in the dark and not fear it. He wanted them to realize the power of their own minds. To be forever **reliant** on the gods and at their mercy was a terrible fate.

As Prometheus watched from his ledge, the rain suddenly stopped. "Zeus must have gotten tired of his silly games," thought Prometheus.

He stood up and brushed off his robe. A chilly wind blew through him. Winter was on its way, with its cold blasts. His beloved humans couldn't last another season without fire.

Prometheus finally left the cold cliff and went home. But all that night he tossed and turned, worrying. What could he do? By morning light, he knew. He went to talk to Zeus.

The powerful god did not take Prometheus' request well. "Absolutely not!" he roared. "Give humans fire? Why? They're happy without it."

"You call that happy?" Prometheus protested as he pointed below. "Look at them! They're cold and unclothed.

[3] (zūs)

They have few weapons with which to kill beasts or protect themselves. What little food they can **scavenge**, they must eat raw. And they lose their way in the dark! Would you wish for such a *happy* life, Zeus?''

Zeus snorted. ''Prometheus, you're supposed to be so wise. Don't you know that humans would become miserable with fire? Each gift comes at a price. That is fate. If I gave humans fire, they'd create more weapons. Then they'd begin a system of **commerce**. Soon one human would have more than the next. Envy and greed would be born, and wars would follow.''

Zeus shook his head. ''No, leave the humans to me, Prometheus. I know what's best.''

Zeus turned his back on Prometheus. As far as the mighty god was concerned, the discussion had closed.

But Prometheus wasn't willing to give up so easily. He stepped in front of Zeus and tried another **tactic**.

''Of what purpose is this human race if they are to live like beasts?''

Zeus answered impatiently. ''So they can worship us, Prometheus. *That* is why I allowed you to create them. To offer us sacrifices. Though as you well know, they get the best of that bargain!''

This last thought caused Zeus to glare at Prometheus. He still recalled Prometheus' part in the division of the sacrifices. Long ago a meeting had been held to decide how sacrifices should be shared. When an animal was killed, it was understood that part should be offered to the gods. But which part?

Prometheus had volunteered to help decide the question. ''I'll divide the meat into portions,'' he said. As Zeus stared suspiciously, Prometheus hastily added, ''Then you, of course, shall choose the gods' share.''

Zeus was right to be suspicious. Prometheus had cleverly gathered the rich meat from an ox and wrapped it in some tough hide. But as for the bones, he hid them in a tempting layer of fat. Then he invited Zeus to choose which share the gods desired. Zeus picked the **deceptive** bundle of fat and bones.

Then how the heavens shook when Zeus discovered the trick! No, Zeus wouldn't soon forget or forgive Prometheus' plan. In fact, since that time Zeus had angrily denied humans most comforts. Especially fire.

Now Prometheus quickly tried to change the subject. He decided to appeal to Zeus' anger instead of his good will.

"But great lord of the sky, wouldn't humans be much more amusing with fire?" the Titan suggested. "Imagine them blundering into the flames. Or how frightened they would be at the sight of their own shadows. Think of the endless possibilities."

Zeus smiled. He knew Prometheus was trying to trick him.

"Fire might make humans more amusing," he replied. "But it would surely make them more dangerous. You may have noticed a few of their worst qualities. Pride, for one. They need very little **provocation** to become boastful toads. If we give them fire. . . . Well, forget about **humility** or devotion. With fire, they'll think they're gods. They might even try to take over Olympus."

Zeus frowned at the thought. "Dangerous, indeed. Perhaps I'll just squash this human race before they even get such ideas. Maybe then your loyalties will return to the gods, where they belong."

Prometheus started to protest, but Zeus angrily shook his head. "No more! I will not allow you to give your precious humans fire! Now be gone, Prometheus."

With that, Zeus stormed out of the room. Prometheus guessed he was probably on his way to brew more rain clouds. Prometheus remained standing where he was, deep in thought. He knew humans had no future on earth without fire. So there was only one thing to do.

That night Prometheus crept into an empty hall on Olympus. In this hall, the gods' central fire blazed.

Quietly, Prometheus pulled out a hollow reed. After a quick glance around, he reached into the fire and brought out a coal.

"A jewel fit for my humans," Prometheus whispered to himself. Carefully the **rebellious** god placed the nugget inside the reed.

Before leaving, Prometheus took one last look at Olympus. He knew he'd never be allowed back. Then he turned and began his **descent** to earth.

A god moves with the swiftness of thought. So in several moments, Prometheus touched ground. Then he began his search.

The Titan soon found what he was looking for. At the entrance to a cave, he stopped and knelt in the sand. As the night winds peered curiously over his shoulder, Prometheus dug a shallow pit. Then he gathered dry brush from around the cave and put it in the pit. Finally he topped the brush with a few pieces of wood.

By this time, a few shadowy figures had appeared at the mouth of the cave. They did not speak. They simply watched in **awe**.

"The bed is ready," Prometheus murmured. "Now for my sleeping coal."

So saying, Prometheus took his reed and split it apart. The red coal fell into the pit. Instantly a tiny flame rose.

Prometheus leaned down and blew softly on the young fire. The flames grew fatter, snapping as they widened. Finally a circle of light surrounded Prometheus and his friends.

Prometheus glanced up and smiled at the humans. He gestured for them to come closer.

One by one they came out of the cave and crouched by the fire. But when they felt its great warmth, they jumped back in alarm.

"Don't be frightened," Prometheus **soothed** them. "This is called fire. Sit at just the right distance and it will keep back the cold without burning you."

The humans moved back to the fire and whispered quietly among themselves.

"Now to show you its other powers," Prometheus said. "Aha!" he exclaimed as he spotted a freshly killed deer at the cave entrance. "Tonight you shall dine like the kings you will be!"

Prometheus cut a piece of the meat and placed it on a stick over the flame. The hungry flames cracked and smacked as the fat oozed down. The humans were hungry, too. Prometheus could see their mouths watering.

When the meat was finished cooking, the god held it out to them. A tall man took the hot meat and bit it eagerly.

"Ahhhhhhh!!" he screamed in pain. As Zeus had warned, gifts come at a price. The man had burned his tongue.

Prometheus quickly calmed the startled humans. "This fire can change your whole life. But you must learn how to **tend** it. You must feed it many twigs or it will die. But don't feed it too much or it will **devour** everything in sight. Even you! If it escapes your circle, throw water on it. Fire fears water and will fade at its touch."

Prometheus pulled the man eating the deer meat into the circle. He showed the man how to start a fire and **coax** it into flames. Soon the second fire had grown to a healthy golden blaze.

The man smiled at Prometheus.

That night and for many others, Prometheus went from cave to cave. Everywhere he went, he carried a live coal and the secret of fire. Finally every human knew how to light, feed, and put out a fire.

Prometheus also passed on other gifts to the young race. He showed humans the mysteries of writing, healing, shipbuilding, metalworking, and animal herding.

All went well until one day when Zeus spotted tiny lights on the earth below. He took a closer look and noticed humans cooking their food with fires. He saw huts, farmhouses, and villages. He saw blacksmith shops. He saw people clothed in skins and wool. He saw fields of corn and

fleets of boats. He saw warriors holding spears and riding in chariots, just like gods.

Zeus was furious. "By the heavens, I can guess who's responsible for this!" he bellowed. "Well, Prometheus, if man wants fire so much, I'll give him fire!"

Zeus raised his mighty arm. He was fully prepared to set the whole earth ablaze.

Then a thought struck him, and he lowered his arm. "No," he said to himself. "I'll have my revenge. And I'll have my entertainment, too. Humans will destroy themselves with this new-found gift. It will make for a long, amusing game." Zeus smiled grimly.

"But as for you, Prometheus . . . . It is time for your little tricks to come to an end!"

Zeus clapped his hands and two huge guards appeared at his side. Zeus instructed them to find the rebellious Prometheus and take him to the Caucasus[4] Mountains. Then Zeus summoned his son, Hephaestus.[5]

Hephaestus limped into his father's presence. "Yes, Father?" he asked. "You sent for me?"

Zeus gazed at his odd son. Of all the gods, Hephaestus was the only one who wasn't beautiful. In fact, Hephaestus was ugly and crippled.

Yet the gods respected Hephaestus' skills. He was the best metalworker in the universe. He'd created shields, armor, jewelry—even lifelike figures that moved by themselves.

But now his father had a distasteful task for him. "I need your strongest chains, Hephaestus. Chains to bind the rebel Prometheus! Fetch your tools and follow me," he ordered.

Zeus and Hephaestus set off at once for the Caucasus Mountains. There they found Prometheus under guard.

Zeus glared. "You went against my will, Prometheus," he spoke sternly. "You gave humans a secret of the gods! For that, you will be bound to this rock forever. No rest, no company, no food. Indeed, *you* will be the food!"

[4](ko' ka sus or kaw' ka sus)
[5](he fes' tus)

He waved his hand and a vulture appeared. The bird gave a hungry cry as it **hovered** overhead.

Zeus pointed at the sky. "Every day that vulture will tear out your liver. And every day your liver will grow back. Every day to the end of time, Prometheus. Now let your brave humans save you! If there are any around after I'm finished with them!"

Zeus vanished in a clap of thunder.

In the silence that followed, Hephaestus turned to Prometheus. "Please, my friend. I don't do this willingly, but—"

"But do it you must," Prometheus softly finished for him. "I foresaw my fate, Hephaestus. I knew what the outcome was to be. And I accepted it."

With that, the Titan stretched himself out on the rock. Hephaestus gave a mighty sigh and knelt beside him. Then the god of the forge took up his hammer, spikes, and chains and set to work.

Quietly he did his duty. Yet as he prepared to drive in the last spike, he paused. "For all eternity, Prometheus! How can I do this? How can you bear it?"

Prometheus raised his handsome head. "As I told you, Hephaestus, I foresaw this. Now I foresee an end to it as well. And Zeus himself will permit me to be freed. For I have a secret, Hephaestus. The most important secret in the universe to the great god of the sky," he said.

"A secret?" whispered Hephaestus.

But Prometheus' only answer was a smile. He wasn't going to tell anyone, including Hephaestus, about the lovely Thetis.[6] Thetis' son was **destined** to be greater than his father, no matter who his father was. Even if Zeus were the father, Thetis' son would still be greater.

"All in good time, Hephaestus," Prometheus replied at last. "You'll know in thirty years. Or is it thirty thousand? But when the day comes that Zeus gives in, both I and the secret shall be set free."

[6] (thē′ tis)

Prometheus settled back as Hephaestus drove in the last spike. Yes, he would lie here in pain for years upon years. But he had **defied** the gods and given his beloved humans a future. For despite Zeus' threats, humans would survive. Then some day, one of the greatest of them all would set him free.

INSIGHTS

Prometheus' name means *forethought*. With his power to foresee the future, he helped save humans from total destruction.

The story goes that Zeus grew angry at the evils of the human race. Therefore, he decided to wipe out the entire race by sending a terrible rainstorm. The storm flooded the world and killed everyone.

Everyone, that is, except Prometheus' own son and daughter-in-law. This couple, Deucalion and Pyrrha, escaped by floating in a large wooden chest.

As Prometheus foresaw, Zeus took pity on these two good souls. He drained the land and helped them start a new race of humans.

Prometheus could live forever only if some immortal would trade places with him. This seemed unlikely until the centaur Chiron was wounded by a poisoned arrow. (Centaurs were half-man, half-horse.) Since he was in great pain, Chiron begged to take Prometheus' spot in Hades. In turn, Prometheus was given a permanent place on Olympus.

Prometheus was able to comfort the woman who eventually helped free him. This woman, Io, had been changed into a cow by her lover, Zeus. Zeus had transformed Io to keep his wife, Hera, from knowing about the affair.

Of course, jealous Hera guessed the truth. She took revenge by sending a stinging fly to chase the woman/cow.

As she fled from the fly, Io met Prometheus while he lay chained to the rocks. He comforted Io by predicting that she would soon be returned to human form. He also knew that Io was carrying Zeus' child, who would become a great king. This was happy news to Prometheus. For one day, a relative of this king would free Prometheus.

Some legends say Hephaestus was lame because his father, Zeus, threw him off Olympus. The place where Hephaestus landed was the island of Lemnos. This island became the center of the god's worship. In time, mostly blacksmiths lived there.

Hephaestus' own workshop was on Olympus. There he turned out many wonders. For Achilles and Aeneas, he created armor. For Heracles and Agamemnon, he crafted shields. He even made Aeetes' fire-breathing bulls.

Hephaestus also fashioned wonders for the gods. He made them brass houses, golden shoes, and marvelous chariots. He shoed their horses, too.

For himself, he made two golden "robots." These two women helped the lame god walk.

Many great works have been inspired by Prometheus' story. Aeschylus' play *Prometheus Bound,* Shelley's play *Prometheus Unbound,* and Byron's poem "Prometheus" are among the retellings of the tale.

THE TWELVE LABORS OF HERACLES

VOCABULARY PREVIEW

Below is a list of words that appear in the story. Read the list and get to know the words before you start the story.

agitated—disturbed; restless
deter—discourage or scare off
distract—draw attention away; sidetrack
foul—disgusting
gaped—stared in surprise
glumly—sadly
infuriated—made angry
intruder—unwelcome guest; invader
mulled—thought over; considered carefully
murky—dark and cloudy
oracle—person, place, or method for consulting the gods; source of wisdom and truth
penance—act done to make up for a sin; punishment taken
protruding—sticking out
quivered—trembled; shook
reverence—honor; deep respect
sear—burn to a crisp
stature—size; height
suffice—to be enough
tyrannical—unjust; without mercy
wary—cautious; very careful

THE
TWELVE LABORS
OF
HERACLES

The circus strongman in
his animal-skin leotard has a
distant cousin in Greek myth.
In fact, that "relative" is one
of Greece's greatest heroes:
Heracles. (The Romans called
him Hercules.) Like those
circus strongmen, Heracles
was known for his animal-skin
cloak and his fabulous strength.
With that strength, Heracles
performed twelve of the
hardest deeds in the history
of myth.

What could the strongest man in the world
have to fear?

Strong or not, every sensible Greek feared and
respected the gods. Even Heracles,[1] the strongest
man among all the Greek heroes.

[1] (her′ a klēz)

Heracles had to be particularly **wary** of Hera, Zeus' queen.[2] This powerful goddess was always jealous of her husband's lovers and the children they bore him. So naturally she hated Heracles, who was the son of Zeus and the mortal woman Alcmene.[3]

From the day he was born, Hera declared war on Heracles. While he was still a babe in the crib, she sent two serpents to kill him. But Heracles was quick. He seized the serpents with his chubby little hands and choked the life out of them.

From that day on, Heracles' family knew he had a great role to play. So they tried to prepare him for it. He was taught everything by the masters of each skill. He learned how to shoot with a bow and arrow. He perfected his fighting abilities and learned how to drive a chariot. He also trained to play the lyre[4] and sing.

While he was mastering his lessons, Heracles continued to grow at an amazing rate. He was soon much stronger and taller than other young men.

But with this strength and **stature** came a hot temper. This was a deadly mix, as it soon turned out. One day Heracles argued with his music teacher. The teacher found fault with Heracles and hit him. Heracles' face instantly turned a fierce red. Enraged, he picked up the harp, struck the man, and killed him.

Heracles was not accused of murder since the teacher had struck first. But after the incident, he was sent to work on a cattle farm. Heracles' family knew he would master great things in the future. But they also knew he first had to master his temper.

While at the farm, Heracles killed a lion who had been slaughtering cattle. He also gathered an army of men from Thebes[5] and led a battle against the king of a nearby city. This king had held the city of Thebes under his thumb.

[2](her′ a   or   hē′ ra) (zūs)
[3](alk mē′ ne)
[4]A lyre is a small stringed instrument of the harp family.
[5](thēbz)

Heracles won the battle and set the people of Thebes free. The King of Thebes, Creon,[6] was so happy with Heracles that he allowed his daughter to marry the hero.

For a time afterwards, Heracles enjoyed a glorious life. But Hera was standing by, still ready to destroy him at any chance. After Heracles and his wife had a few children, Hera saw her chance. The cruel goddess struck the hero with madness. And in that madness, Heracles killed his wife and children.

When Heracles came to his senses and saw what he had done, he dropped to his knees. "Oh mighty gods!" he wept. "Why have you made me do this? How can I ever cleanse my bloody hands of this deed?"

The answer came to Heracles as clearly as if Zeus himself spoke: "Go to Delphi."[7]

So Heracles quickly set off for the great god Apollo's[8] **oracle.** Once there, Heracles learned from the oracle that to make up for the crime, he must serve Eurystheus[9] for twelve years. Heracles was to perform any service that this prince of Mycenae[10] asked of him.

Heracles obeyed and immediately sought out Eurystheus. Little did the hero realize that Hera was already ahead of him. She had visited Eurystheus and found him eager to bring Heracles' downfall. The prince had heard tales of the brave, handsome Heracles and burned with jealousy. He was only too happy to plan twelve impossible labors or tasks for Heracles. The tasks would be so dangerous that no one could survive them.

Heracles didn't know of these plots. Yet he did know from the minute he met the prince that they wouldn't get along. Heracles eyed Eurystheus as the prince leaned back in his lovely throne. Many guards stood close by, ready to do all the prince's fighting for him.

[6](krē' on)
[7](del' fī)
[8](a pol' lō)
[9](ū ris' thūs or ū ris' thē us)
[10](mi sē' nē)

Heracles couldn't respect a man like that. But it was his **penance** to serve Eurystheus. So serve him he would.

Heracles swallowed his disgust. "Prince, I humble myself to do your will," he said. "I'll do whatever you command."

Eurystheus stared at Heracles and grinned. Heracles hated him even more.

"Excellent, Heracles. I do have a few things I want you to undertake."

Again the prince paused and smiled. "First, a small thing. I want you to bring back the skin of the lion of Nemea.[11] It's nothing like the animal you supposedly killed in your cattle farming days. Bring me its skin. At once."

Eurystheus chuckled as Heracles set out on his task with bow and arrows and a heavy club. What the scheming prince didn't tell Heracles was the secret of the lion's strength.

Heracles didn't stop to rest until he got to the thick wood of Nemea. There he met an old man on the path.

"Good day, fellow," Heracles said. "Could you tell me where the great lion lives?"

The old man shook at the mention of the lion.

"Never fear. I'm here to kill him," Heracles quickly added.

The old man took a closer look at the body towering over him. "Heracles?"

"Yes, I'm Heracles. And I'm here to help your city."

At this, the old man's eyes brightened. He eagerly pointed his wrinkled finger toward the thickest part of the forest.

"At nightfall, I see him coming from there."

"Ah. Many thanks, old fellow."

Fearless Heracles was off at once. Without any hesitation, he marched into the dark wood.

Long after nightfall, Heracles stopped in front of a cave. He thought if he were a lion, he'd make his den in there. And sure enough, as Heracles cautiously entered, he found the remains of a deer. Heracles tucked himself behind a rock and waited.

[11] (nem′ ē a or nē mē′ a)

Before dawn, the lion padded into his den and plopped his huge body down. He yawned and slowly licked his bloody mouth.

Suddenly, the lion raised his nose to the air. Something was different.

At once Heracles leapt from his hiding place and shot an arrow straight at the beast. To his astonishment, he saw it slide off the tough hide.

The lion gave an angry growl and spun toward Heracles. Quickly, Heracles let loose another arrow. This time, he hit the beast directly in the chest. But again the arrow bounced to the ground.

The lion's eyes narrowed. Giving a savage roar, it sprang!

As it rushed forward, Heracles raised his club. With a loud crack, he brought it down on the lion's head.

Then the hero **gaped** at what he saw. The club had shattered into a hundred pieces.

But the blow managed to stun the lion for a brief moment. In that moment, Heracles realized what the prince hadn't told him. This lion could not be hurt by weapons.

With a roar as loud as the lion's, Heracles threw himself on the huge animal's back. Though the lion tried to claw and bite him, Heracles locked his hands round its throat. Finally he succeeded in choking the beast to death.

Heracles stared at his prize.

"Well, the beast's dead," he said to himself. "But the job's only half done. How do I get that tough hide off of him?"

Then Heracles spied the lion's claw. Would that do the job?

He grabbed the claw and pierced the skin. It worked!

When Heracles returned to Eurystheus' palace, he wore the lion's skin on his back. With the lion's head as a helmet and its front paws draped over his chest, Heracles looked truly fierce.

At least Eurystheus thought so. He took one look at Heracles and ran in the other direction. Heracles roared with laughter.

"What's the matter, prince? Never seen a lion-man before?"

Eurystheus peeked from behind a door. His angry glare gave way to a cruel grin. The next labor was certain to stop Heracles' laughter.

"Get on with your work," the prince ordered. "Kill me the Hydra!"[12]

A deadly assignment, Heracles thought. The Hydra had nine snakelike heads, and the middle one was immortal. No one had ever been able to destroy the creature. It seemed impossible when every time you cut off a head, two more grew.

Heracles set off on this labor with his nephew, Iolaus.[13] They drove their chariot long and far until they reached the Hydra's swamp.

Heracles slowly waded into the **murky** water. "Come, monster!" he called. "Here's another meal for you."

The Hydra eagerly accepted the invitation. In one great spring, it leapt out of the water straight at the hero.

Heracles backed away and shot arrow after arrow at the creature. But as each head dropped, two more rose up. The Hydra was becoming stronger, not weaker!

"Iolaus! My club! Get me my club!"

Iolaus grabbed the heavy club and dragged it to Heracles. Heracles lifted it easily into the air and swung at the creature. Faster and faster he whirled the club. He smashed the Hydra's heads so quickly, they barely had time to grow back before the next blow fell.

But angry Hera was looking on. She was furious that once again Heracles seemed about to triumph. So she sent a crab to help the Hydra.

[12] (hī' dra)
[13] (ī ō lā' us)

The sharp nip of that tiny creature was enough to **distract** Heracles. He glanced down and crushed the crab before it could attack again. But when he looked back at the Hydra, it was ready for him. In that short time, the creature had recovered. It now had hundreds of heads.

Heracles stepped back. "Iolaus, this club won't kill it. I need—" Heracles thought quickly. "I need a fire! Build me a fire, quick as you can! I'll be back."

When Heracles returned, he carried a branding iron. He stuffed the iron deep into the embers and waited.

"Nephew, I need your help. I'll cut off each head. As I do that, **sear** each neck with this red-hot iron."

And that is exactly what they did. As Heracles chopped off a head, Iolaus seared the neck so the head could not grow back. Finally, Heracles cut off the immortal head and buried it under a mountain. What was left of the dead Hydra sank back into the dark swamp.

Heracles' third labor was to fetch the stag sacred to the goddess Artemis.[14] This stag was a beautiful snow-white. It also had golden antlers and brass hoofs.

Eurystheus knew Artemis loved this stag. He was counting on her to stop Heracles.

Heracles set off. For a whole year he chased the beautiful stag. Finally, they were both so exhausted, they landed in a heap not far from each other.

At that moment, Artemis appeared. With a grim look on her face, she drew her bow. She pointed the arrow straight at Heracles.

"How dare you cross me!" the goddess exclaimed. "I have only to release my fingers and you will die. So leave this place, Heracles. I will not allow anyone to chase my stag."

Heracles knew the angry goddess had killed other mortals before. He would have to do something quickly if he didn't want to be added to the list.

[14](ar' te mis)

"Dear goddess, I never intended to hurt this pretty animal. But it's Eurystheus' wish to see him. As soon as that's done, I'll return your stag to this very spot. I swear it."

Artemis looked into Heracles' heart and saw he was telling the truth. At last she nodded.

With a relieved smile, Heracles led the stag away. Then true to his word, as soon as Prince Eurystheus saw the animal, Heracles returned it to the goddess.

The fourth labor was to capture the great boar of Erymanthus.[15] This boar could outrun a horse. And it had long sharp tusks **protruding** from its nose. Many a person had died on those tusks.

Heracles chased the great boar over the plains, into the valleys, and through the mountains.

At last he stopped. "Fool," Heracles scolded himself. "I may have the feet of a deer but my brain is a turtle. I can never outrun this beast. It's even stronger than that stag. Something to slow it down is what I need."

Just then Heracles spotted a mountaintop white with snow. "Those drifts will take the fire out of his hoofs," Heracles said with a weary grin.

At once Heracles began driving the beast up the mountain. As the hero guessed, the boar slowed when it reached the heavy snow. At last it bogged down completely.

Heracles closed in and threw some chains over the boar. Then he heaved the beast onto his shoulders. "Another prize for my prince, the coward," he muttered. Then with a grin, he set off for Mycenae.

Eurystheus gritted his teeth when he saw Heracles return. But he was soon ready with another task.

"Some housework, this time, Heracles," the prince said. "Or more accurately, a little housecleaning for cows. You should relate well to them."

The hero frowned. Heracles might joke about his own intelligence. But he resented it when others made fun of him.

[15] (er i man' thus)

Eurystheus saw the frown and quickly went on. "Your fifth labor is to clean the stables of King Augeas.[16] A day should **suffice**."

A day! Heracles didn't know whether to laugh or bellow. Augeas' stables housed 30,000 head of cattle. And the stables hadn't been cleaned in thirty years. The floors were caked with filth and grime.

"So you think you have me beaten, eh, Eurystheus? We'll see." Determined Heracles traveled to Elis.[17] Once there, he sat down on a high hill above the stables.

For a long while he thought about his task. As he stared at the landscape, the glint of water caught his eye. A river. Two rivers!

An idea slowly took shape in Heracles' head. Then with a great laugh, he strode down to the stables and broke down part of the walls at both ends. After grabbing a shovel, he went outside and began digging a ditch.

Steadily the hero dug. Only now and again did he glance up to see that he was on course.

At last Heracles reached the banks of the first river. With a final shovel, he connected his ditch to the river. Then he dug another ditch to the second river.

The water eagerly flowed from the two river beds. Right through the huge building the streams ran. In no time at all, the walls and floors were sparkling clean.

The sixth labor set upon Heracles was to destroy the birds of Stymphalus.[18] This huge flock of birds lived in a marsh near Mycenae. The **foul** birds carried terrible diseases and tore the flesh off any living creature.

Heracles carefully made his way over the bones and skulls of people and animals. " 'Harmless birds' did you say, Eurystheus?" Heracles grumbled. "Maybe for you. What creature would want your bitter flesh?"

Finally Heracles could go no farther without sinking

[16](o′ jē as)
[17](ē′ lis)
[18](stim fā′ lus)

into the stinking marsh. "Now how to get to those birds? Can I plow my way through?"

Luckily, Athena[19] came to his aid. The great warrior goddess stirred the wind, shaking some marsh pods. These pods made a rattling sound.

"Aha, goddess Athena. That rattle you gave me. How could I have forgotten?" Heracles said.

He reached into a bag at his side and drew out a brass rattle which Athena had given him. Then he moved to a mountainside near the marsh and shook the deafening rattle.

At that sound, the startled birds rose above the marsh. They soon spotted the noisemaker. At once the flock moved in to attack.

Faster than a whipping wind, Heracles loaded his bow. Arrow upon arrow he shot. Yet though he killed many birds, more appeared and joined the attack.

Again Athena helped the hero by placing an invisible shield over Heracles. This shield protected him from the birds' hooked beaks and clawed feet.

Heracles continued to launch arrows. He shot one after another until his bow was smoking. Finally not a bird was left alive in the marsh.

Victory brought no rest for the hero. Heracles' seventh labor was to bring the Cretan[20] bull to Eurystheus. This bull had been a gift to King Minos from Poseidon, god of the sea.[21] Minos had promised to sacrifice the bull on Poseidon's altar. But as soon as he received the beautiful white animal, Minos had hidden it away.

Now anyone knows a god cannot be deceived. Poseidon took revenge on Minos by striking the bull with madness. After that, no wall or fence could hold the beast. The people were terrified of him.

Heracles knew these tales about the bull. Yet they didn't **deter** him. He sailed to the island of Crete and calmly began searching for the bull.

[19] (a thē′ na)
[20] (krē′ tan)
[21] (mī′ nos) (pō sī′ don)

Before long, Heracles found the animal.

"Come, pet," he called. "We've a little trip to take."

The bull snorted angrily and charged. At the last moment, Heracles grabbed its horns and leapt onto its back.

The bull roared and began bucking. But strong Heracles held on, gripping the bull all the tighter.

Hour after hour they spun. Night fell and still the dance continued.

Then as day broke, the bull gave a huge sigh and sank to the ground.

Heracles patted its broad head. "I told you, pet. We've a trip to take." He loaded the bull onto his back and headed back to Mycenae.

Heracles' eighth task was to fetch the man-eating mares of Diomedes.[22] Diomedes was the **tyrannical** king of Thrace.[23] His people lived in constant fear of being seized and fed to the mares.

Before Heracles left, he again asked Iolaus to join him. When some of Heracles' friends found out, they gathered and approached the hero.

"We'd like to help you rid Thrace of Diomedes," they said.

Heracles gazed off into the distance for a moment. Then he turned back with a huge grin. "Welcome," he said simply.

The group marched to Thrace and immediately captured Diomedes. Then they paraded him in front of the people of Thrace.

"Friends, I've heard about your king's many cruel acts," Heracles said to them. "I'd rather not believe they're true. So if anyone has a kind word to say about Diomedes, speak up."

Complete silence followed.

Heracles continued. "No one, eh? Well, *we* won't punish this man for his crimes. If the tales are true, his own mares will give him the justice he deserves."

[22] (dī ō mē′ dēz)
[23] (thrās)

Heracles led the Thracians to the valley where the mares were kept. There he forced the trembling Diomedes into the pen. Instantly the mares surrounded their former master. They kicked and bit and finally feasted upon his flesh.

When the horror was over, the mares shook themselves. Then they gently trotted over to Heracles. To all appearances, they seemed grateful to be rid of their wicked master.

Now that he was close enough, Heracles saw the mares' condition. "Why, the creatures are starving! Look at their ribs!"

He turned to his men. "Gather some grain and hay and feed these mares at once."

Once that was done, the mares were completely tame. Heracles was able to deliver them to Eurystheus without further trouble.

The ninth labor was to bring back the belt of Hippolyta, queen of the Amazons.[24] Eurystheus hoped that the trip to the Amazons' distant land would be the end of Heracles. But Heracles and his crew arrived safely.

Heracles greeted Hippolyta with **reverence**. He admired this nation made up solely of women. The Amazons were fierce hunters and fighters. Yet they were wise and fair-minded as well.

For their part, the Amazons knew of Heracles. Who didn't? News of Eurystheus' tasks had traveled even to their distant land. They were impressed by Heracles' courage and his ability to do the impossible.

Heracles accepted the Amazons' praise. He also welcomed their invitation to join them for dinner.

As they feasted that night, the Greeks and Amazons exchanged tall tales. Heracles also explained his latest task. Hippolyta listened with respect. When he finished, she gladly offered her belt.

But Hera was watching. The fact that Heracles had succeeded in all his other tasks **infuriated** her. The goddess

[24](hip pol' i ta) (am' a zonz)

wasn't about to let him win the belt so easily.

Hera took the form of an Amazon and entered the feasting hall. From group to group she went. "Warriors," she said in a low voice, "don't be fooled by this fool. His real mission here is to kidnap our queen. Gather your spears. See that he and his men don't leave this hall alive!"

Hera clouded the senses of the women. They believed her and grew furious. With a shout, they launched an attack on the Greeks.

Heracles didn't even stop to think. When he was attacked, he fought back. And he fought to win.

In the fierce battle that followed, Heracles killed Hippolyta. As he saw her sink to the ground, the shock awoke him.

With a groan of regret, the hero grabbed the queen's belt. Then he shouted, "To the ship!"

The Greeks charged for the door and managed to escape. Sad but safe, they sailed to Mycenae.

Scarcely had Heracles touched dry ground before Eurystheus sent him out on his tenth task. This time he was to bring back the oxen of Geryon.[25]

Heracles **mulled** over his task. "Geryon's a monster with three bodies joined at the waist. He has a two-headed dog and a giant herdsman to help guard those cattle of his. And he lives at the ends of the earth."

The mighty hero scratched his chin. "Ah, well. Just so long as there are no more decent people involved. Killing a noble warrior like Hippolyta is one thing. But what's another three monsters?"

Heracles began his long journey to Geryon's island off Spain. For the voyage, he'd borrowed a special magic ship from Helios,[26] the god of the sun.

When he finally reached the island, the fight began at once. Geryon's two-headed dog appeared first. Heracles slew the beast after a short, wild battle.

[25] (jē' ri on or ger' i on)
[26] (hē' li os)

Hardly had he wiped his club than the giant herdsman was upon him. This battle took longer, though Heracles again triumphed.

Finally Geryon himself stepped forward to fight the hero. "Kill my servants, will you!" he screamed from his three heads.

The monster snapped trees from their roots and hurled them at Heracles. With his six huge hands, he also gathered boulders.

Heracles' rapid bow work saved him once again. Quickly he sent three poisoned arrows straight at each body. Perfect hits! The monster crashed to the ground and died.

Now no one was left to stop Heracles from fulfilling his mission. So he drove the oxen into his boat and headed back to the palace.

At the sight of the returning hero, Eurystheus grew very **agitated**. "No! He's won again. Ah, I'd gladly have sacrificed the whole herd to be rid of that one great ox. There must be something that will finish him off!" he moaned.

From behind him, a beautiful but cold voice answered. "There is, Eurystheus."

The prince whirled to find Hera glaring at him. "This time, tell him you have a taste for apples . . . "

Several minutes later, Eurystheus greeted Heracles with a wicked smile.

"I have your eleventh task ready. You will bring me the Golden Apples of the Hesperides."[27]

Heracles gaped. "Prince, that is impossible!" he finally protested. "No one knows where the apples are."

Eurystheus chuckled. Heracles thought he heard a woman laughing somewhere, too.

"So you wish to defy me, Heracles? You wish to go against my orders? Ah, well, I knew you would fail me."

Heracles looked away for a moment. He had already completed ten impossible tasks. And for a sniveling coward!

[27](hes per' i dēz)

Well, if a coward thought he could wear out a son of Zeus . . .

Heracles stepped closer. "I won't fail you. I'll return with the apples."

But under his breath, Heracles muttered, "Wherever they may be." He nodded to Eurystheus and left.

For all his brave words, the hero felt confused. Where was he to go? Where was he to begin? All he knew was that the three Hesperides lived in a distant garden. A mighty dragon helped them guard the Golden Apples.

"I'll just begin looking," Heracles decided. "Perhaps the gods will see fit to give me directions." So saying, he sailed from Greece.

One day as he coasted near the shore, Heracles heard the cries of a man. Heracles swiftly landed and followed the cries to the top of a mountain. There he found Prometheus, the brave Titan who had defied the gods.[28] He now lay chained to a spiked peak, groaning as a vulture plucked at his liver.

Heracles' hand went to his bow at once. With one shot, he struck the vulture and finished the brave Titan's torture. Then he broke the chains and helped Prometheus to stand.

"Steady there, my friend," Heracles gently said.

"For year upon year I have waited for you," panted the Titan. "At last, Heracles."

"You know me then?" Heracles asked. "Well, I know you. You must be Prometheus, the Titan who gave humans fire. From the stories I've heard, Zeus didn't approve of that. Yes, my father really must have been angry to chain you up like this. And people think I have a temper!" Heracles laughed.

"I think you've suffered enough, Prometheus," he added. "It's time for you to be free and see how we humans have got on. I'd say we've done quite well. Thanks to you, that is."

---

[28] (prō mē thūs or prō mē′ thē us)(tī′ tan) Titans were a race of powerful gods. Most were punished for their part in a war against Zeus. Prometheus aided Zeus in the war but later offended the god.

A quiet, proud smile came to Prometheus' face. Then he searched Heracles' eyes. "But what of the gods? What of Zeus?"

"I respect the gods," said Heracles. "Yes, I even fear them. But not even to please the gods will I be a worm. So if the gods don't like it—any of them—they can take up the matter with me."

Again Prometheus smiled proudly. "Thank you, Heracles. I knew one day there would come a hero brave enough to challenge the gods. I'm happy to have met him. Now tell me of your travels. I guess that there is a purpose behind your wandering."

Heracles explained his mission to Prometheus.

Prometheus nodded after Heracles finished. "I may be able to help you, my friend. I suggest you ask my fellow Titan, Atlas.[29] Since he is the father of the Hesperides, he will know where the apples are."

Heracles thanked him and they bid each other farewell. But before Prometheus was out of sight, Heracles shouted after him.

"I forgot to ask! Where can I find Atlas?"

"You can't miss him! He's the great figure to the north holding up the sky!"

Just as Prometheus said, Heracles soon found the huge Titan. On his broad shoulders he bore the heavens. This was his punishment for joining a revolt against the gods.

Heracles leaned back and stared up at the giant. In his loudest voice, he roared his tale and request to Atlas.

Atlas' voice boomed back. "I cannot tell you where the Golden Apples are. Yet I may be persuaded to get them for you."

"Yes?" Heracles waited.

"Yes. In fact, I'll fetch them right now. If you'll take the heavens from my shoulders."

Heracles thought a moment. Then he shouted, "Agreed!"

[29] (at′ las)

Scarcely had Heracles spoken before Atlas bent down. Onto Heracles' broad shoulders he dropped the entire weight of the heavens.

Heracles gasped when he felt the great weight. His feet sank in the earth and he **quivered**. A few stars shaken by his trembling tumbled from the sky. But Heracles steadied himself and finally mastered the burden.

Now free of that terrible weight, Atlas stretched his arms and legs. Then with a grin and a wave, he quickly set off into the forest.

Soon Atlas reappeared with a basket of the Golden Apples. Heracles sighed in relief when he saw the Titan. His back had begun to ache.

Atlas stopped a distance away and gazed at Heracles. "You know, Heracles, I can deliver these apples as well as you. Why don't you stay and rest your feet?"

Rest his feet! Heracles gulped. He knew Atlas intended to leave and never come back. But Heracles was no more eager to hold up the heavens for all time than Atlas. His knees were already shaking from the strain.

Heracles tried to think fast. "Thanks for the offer, Atlas. You know the way to the prince's palace, don't you? But before you go, could you hold the heavens for a second? I need to scratch my shoulders."

"Well, I suppose so," Atlas said uncertainly.

The Titan bent down and placed the heavens onto his own shoulders. At once Heracles picked up the apples and ran. He didn't stop until he reached the gates to Eurystheus' palace.

Again no one at Mycenae was happy to see Heracles. The prince **glumly** took the apples and marched to a nearby hall. "Great goddess Hera," he wailed.

She was there in an instant. "So, another success for the great hero. Another failure for us. There's only one task left before he's set free, Eurystheus."

"I know, goddess. But what am I to do?" he whined.

"Send him to the one place from which no human—hero or not—ever comes back alive," Hera commanded.

Hope and triumph crept back over Eurystheus' face. "Of course," he whispered.

Back into the hall the prince eagerly went. "One task left, is it Heracles? Hmm. A dog. I'd like a dog. The best guard dog in the world—or the Underworld for that matter. For your twelfth labor, bring me Cerberus,"[30] ordered Eurystheus.

Heracles stared blankly for a moment. This weakling might as well have shouted, "I order you to die!" Fetching the three-headed dog who guarded the land of the dead was a death sentence.

But Heracles didn't even consider refusing. Freedom was too close. And the more he thought about it, the more thrilling the challenge became. To go to Hades[31] and back! Not many heroes could boast of that.

Aloud, Heracles simply said, "As you wish, prince." Then he turned and walked from the room.

With the help of the gods, Heracles found the opening to Hades in a black lake. Taking a huge breath, he dove into the lake and swam.

When Heracles opened his eyes, he was in a black tunnel. A cool breeze lashed his face. The river the gods spoke of—it must be ahead.

It was. And there Heracles found Charon.[32] This old boatman took the dead across the river to Hades.

Heracles shouldered his way through the dead souls waiting to cross. "Greetings, old fellow," he called. "I need your ferry."

Charon stared in disgust at Heracles. "You're still alive! Well, my ferry carries only the dead." The old man started to row away.

"Not today!" Heracles shouted and jumped into the boat.

[30](ser′ ber us)
[31](hā′ dēz) Hades was both the name of the Underworld and the god who ruled it.
[32](ka′ ron)

Charon sat back in shock. Then he began grumbling to himself. "Fool! Hades, king of this place, will punish you. Living folk are not allowed here. And my boat! My boat will sink with your great weight."

Heracles said not a word in return. Like any proper warrior, he was busy checking his weapons. It wouldn't do to be caught in a fight with splintered arrows.

At the far shore, Heracles jumped out and marched up the bank. Waiting for him was the dog he'd been looking for.

Cerberus was ready for the fight. He came spitting and growling with all three of his heads. But the dog stopped short when he saw the **intruder**. Never before had he seen a man—living or dead—of that stature. Cerberus noted, too, the glow in Heracles' eyes and the heavy club in his hand.

Then from Heracles' throat came the mightiest roar Cerberus had ever heard.

The dog immediately turned tail and ran to find his master, Hades.

Heracles charged after Cerberus. Right and left flew the frightened spirits of that place. A few tried to stand up to him. But even Hades' greatest monsters fell beneath Heracles' club.

At last Heracles tracked Cerberus to Hades' throne. He found the dark god waiting for him.

"Why are you here, foolish man?" demanded Hades in a hard voice. "Surely you must know that no one who enters this place leaves?"

Hades' voice sent a chill through Heracles. He hurriedly explained. "Great god, I am here only at the command of my prince. He has ordered me to bring Cerberus to him. It is the last order of his I must follow. Bringing your beast to his gates will free me."

"Your master must be mad—or hateful."

Heracles shrugged. "You are wiser in the ways of humans than I, great lord. But I have sworn to follow his orders as penance. For I killed my wife and children. I can't forgive myself for that.''

Hades nodded knowingly. Heracles realized with a start that his family must be tucked away in some corner of this gloom.

Heracles continued, ''People say I'm a slow learner, great Hades. But by bearing with my master for all these years, I think I've found how to control my temper and strength.''

Heracles stopped and waited humbly for Hades' reply.

The god spoke slowly. ''You have a stronger heart than most humans, Heracles. I admire that. I will let you leave Hades, for you have much more to do in the land of the living. I will also let you take Cerberus—if you promise to return him. He serves me well. I cannot do without him.''

''Thank you, Hades.'' Heracles moved quickly towards the dog.

Hades held up a warning hand. ''He will not go willingly.''

Heracles sighed. ''Then I must teach him how to obey.''

The wrestling match between man and dog lasted for several hours. In the end, Heracles triumphed and led the tamed Cerberus back to earth.

Straight to the palace the two went. Straight to Eurystheus' private quarters.

''Heracles!'' the startled prince exclaimed. ''You've returned from Hades? But no one returns from that place!''

Heracles laughed the laugh of a free man and thrust the dog forward. ''Here's your prize, prince.'' Eurystheus cried out and jumped into a huge vase.

''I hope you got a good look at his eyes!'' Heracles shouted. ''A good, long look. You might have seen a mirror of the blackness inside you. There's plenty of it in this dog's world.''

Eurystheus didn't stir.

''Not interested, my prince?'' Heracles grunted. ''Well, you'll see the place for yourself, soon enough.''

Heracles turned back to the dog. ''Come, Cerberus, let's finish this bargain. I'll take you back to Hades and set you free. Then perhaps at long last, I can set myself free.''

INSIGHTS

Hera cheated Heracles out of his rightful place as ruler. The day Heracles was to be born, Zeus made a promise. He vowed that the relative of Perseus who was born that day would become ruler of Greece. (Perseus was a great hero and the son of Zeus.)

Jealous Hera managed to outfox her husband. She speeded up the birth of another relative of Perseus. Then she slowed Heracles' own. The result was that Heracles was forced to serve this relative. You probably won't be surprised to learn that the relative's name was Eurystheus.

As a young man, Heracles was given a choice. He could select a life of pleasure but also of vice. Or he could face a life of hardship and danger but glory and virtue as well. He chose the latter. This is why choosing virtue over pleasure is sometimes called "the choice of Heracles."

During Heracles' twelve labors, he managed to work in a few extra tasks. He even squeezed in a little fun. While cleaning the Augean stables, he is said to have paused long enough to start the first Olympic Games.

Amazon is derived from *a mazos,* meaning "without breast." According to legend, these women cut off their right breasts in order to draw a bowstring more easily.

Remarkable warriors! And memorable. Once a Spanish explorer fought with a fierce tribe whose women aided the men in battle. In memory of the Greek myth, he named the river where they fought *Amazonas.* Today it is known as the Amazon.

continued

In this myth, Heracles meets up with the famous Titan Atlas. Though Atlas supposedly held up the heavens, he is rarely pictured that way today. This is because later Greeks decided the sky really was not likely to fall. So they began showing Atlas as supporting the great globe earth. After one mapmaker pictured Atlas on the cover of his map book, the word *atlas* was used to mean any book of maps or detailed drawings.

In a strange way, Heracles' trip to Hades was the death of him. While on his mission to fetch Cerberus, Heracles saw the dead hero Meleager. As a kind gesture to Meleager, Heracles promised to marry any of the dead man's sisters.

When he finished his labors, Hades kept his vow by marrying Deianira. Then he and his bride set off for home.

At a river, Heracles asked a centaur named Nessus to carry Deianira across the water. (Centaurs are half-horse, half-man.) Nessus did so. But then, struck by the bride's beauty, he tried to carry her off.

Heracles quickly fired a poisoned arrow at Nessus. As he lay dying, the centaur told Deianira to save some of his blood. He swore that it would act as a love potion. Deianira did so.

Years later, Heracles fell in love with another woman. Desperate to regain her husband's love, Deianira sent him a robe dipped in Nessus' blood.

But Nessus had lied to Deianira. His blood was actually poisoned, not charmed. So when Heracles put on the robe, his flesh was burned.

In terrible pain, Heracles ordered his own funeral fire to be built. Then he cast himself into the flames and died.

Yet for Heracles at least, the story ended happily. Upon his death, he was taken to Olympus. There the angry Hera at last made peace with him. Indeed, she even gave Heracles her daughter Hebe as his bride.

CIRCE AND ODYSSEUS

VOCABULARY PREVIEW

Below is a list of words that appear in the story. Read the list and get to know the words before you start the story.

absorbing—taking in; soaking up
acknowledgment—recognition or agreement
avail—use or benefit
conferred—discussed; consulted
cower—crouch fearfully
defiantly—disobediently; rebelliously
dense—thick; crowded
disembark—go ashore; leave the ship
elapsed—passed by
hazardous—dangerous; risky
hysterical—out of control; wildly upset
impish—devilish; full of pranks
lamenting—grieving; feeling sorrow
lethal—deadly
lots—chances; papers or objects picked at random to determine what action should be taken or who should take it
poised—balanced; steadied
recoiled—jumped back
seer—prophet; adviser
sty—pigpen
sullen—cross; angry

CIRCE and ODYSSEUS

from *THE ODYSSEY*

A great leader must make many decisions. In this myth Odysseus matches wits with the goddess Circe. His actions rescue his men from a strange spell and win the friendship and assistance of the goddess.

What kind of a leader am I?" cried Odysseus.[1] "So many of my men have died on this voyage. I've made the worst enemy imaginable. And now we're lost at sea!"

One of his men tried to comfort him. "It's not completely bad, Odysseus. Look off the bow.[2] There's an island over there, and it looks promising. We can rest, eat, regain our strength, and continue on. We'll make our way home yet."

[1] (ō dis′ ūs or ō dis′ sē us)
[2] The bow is the front part of a ship.

Another man piped up. "You haven't failed us, Odysseus. You were a fearless leader in Troy.[3] Always on the front line of the battle. And we conquered them! We sent those little Trojans packing!" The man grinned at the memory.

"Yes, we've had a bit of trouble at sea!" he continued. "But we'll find Ithaca."[4]

A little man in the corner named Eurylochus[5] mumbled to himself. "A bit of trouble at sea, mate? The Trojan War was over years ago! And we're still trying to get home! We've landed on every island in this blasted Mediterranean Sea except our own! And at every turn we've faced death!

"First, it was that giant, old Cyclops.[6] He decided to have us for dinner. We didn't get out of that one without making the great god of the sea angry. Angry! Why, Poseidon[7] has turned the sea against us ever since that day!

"Oh, we almost had a break when the god of the winds sealed up all the breezes. All except the one from the west. That one he left free to blow us home. But the damn fools I sail with opened the bag of winds. Oh yes, they thought there was gold inside. The winds rushed out, seized our sails, and carried us toward the ends of the earth!"

Eurylochus shook his head. "If that wasn't bad enough, we had to meet up with some more cannibal giants. They ruined our fleet. Left us one ship out of thirteen!

"And now we're about to anchor at another island. The gods know what they've planned for us here. Man-eating plants, maybe? Or huge fish that will rip our throats before we even make it to shore?"

The men didn't hear their grumbling shipmate. They were too busy preparing to **disembark**. Gathering food and wine, they set out for shore.

For two days, Odysseus and his men rested on the island, drinking and **lamenting**.

---

[3] (troi)
[4] (ith′ a ka) Ithaca is a string of islands off the west coast of Greece.
[5] (ū ril′ o kus)
[6] (sī′ klops) The Cyclops was a giant with just one eye.
[7] (pō sī′ don)

On the third day, Odysseus woke to a magnificent dawn. He watched as the sky turned from dark purple to lavender to pink to orange.

When the sun at last lifted above the horizon, Odysseus took his spear and sword. Then he set off for the highest peak he could find.

Odysseus was feeling much stronger. He had wept over the loss of his men, but they weren't all lost. A whole shipful remained. And he wouldn't fail them now. He couldn't.

Odysseus reached a jagged cliff. From there he gazed around the island.

Smoke! Was that smoke? Odysseus stared more closely. Yes, over there tucked deep into the woods was a house. And it was sending up a fat stream of smoke.

Odysseus' immediate reaction was caution. After all the fierce people they'd met, he didn't know what to expect.

Yet he couldn't ignore the hope the house offered. Whoever lived there might be able to give them directions.

Still, it would be risky. Odysseus decided to split his men into two groups and have them draw **lots**. The losers would investigate this odd house.

Odysseus scrambled down the cliff. His plan had filled him with energy. It also set his stomach rumbling. He knew his men were hungry, too.

As if by magic, a deer bounded into sight. Quietly, Odysseus crept up behind the creature and threw his spear. His aim was good, and the deer went down.

Odysseus heaved the beast onto his shoulders and headed back. He reached the shore before any of his men were awake. "Come, my friends!" he shouted. "I say we are not yet lost. Not while we have meat and wine! So let's feast and celebrate. There's still hope!"

The men eagerly gathered round the stag. The sight of a fresh meal set them cheering and slapping each other on the back.

"Hope? Did I hear the word *hope*?" came a voice from the back. Eurylochus pushed his way through the crowd. He stared down at the dead beast.

"That's not hope, my king," he sneered.

"What do you think hope is, Eurylochus?" asked Odysseus.

"A map," he replied in a **sullen** voice.

Another man laughed as he dove into the deer with his knife. "Then you're not as hungry as I am!"

Odysseus and his men hunted some more and then for the rest of the day, they feasted. Even Eurylochus enjoyed a piece of meat. That night they slept well indeed. By morning, they were renewed.

As the men gathered around the morning fires, Odysseus addressed them. "My friends! Yesterday, I saw a house deep in the woods. I think we should pay the owners a visit and see if they can help us. We'll divide into two groups. I'll lead the men on this side of the campfire. Eurylochus, you'll lead those on the other side. Now let's draw lots to see which group will investigate."

The lots were thrown into a helmet. Both men reached in and pulled out a lot. Odysseus opened his fist and smiled. At the same time, Eurylochus groaned.

"Why me? Of all the foolish missions—" Eurylochus grumbled. Then with a loud sigh, he picked up his sword and headed in the direction Odysseus showed. His men followed him into the **dense** woods.

Eurylochus and his group hiked for several hours. At last they came to a clearing, and there stood the house. It was a huge building, made of polished stone.

Obviously someone lived there. For a woman's voice filled the clearing with song.

"I hear a woman singing, Eurylochus," one of the men said.

"Ah, do you? What a sharp one you are," Eurylochus replied. "But more to the point, mate, what do you see?"

He pointed, and the men saw what their leader had already spotted. Mountain lions and wolves were patrolling the entrance.

"All right, who'll play the hero and peek inside?" asked Eurylochus.

One of the men pushed Eurylochus into the clearing. "I think you should do it!"

"Why me?" Eurylochus protested.

"You've got such a happy face. You're sure to win over those beasts!" The men laughed, despite Eurylochus' glare.

Eurylochus walked cautiously toward the house. As quietly as possible, he raised his spear. When the lions and wolves looked up, he **recoiled**. But the beasts remained still.

Eurylochus inched forward again. If he could just get to the door without being attacked.

Then he felt a cold, wet touch on the back of his leg. Eurylochus froze. It took all his courage to turn and see what was behind him.

It was a wolf! But to Eurylochus' relief, the beast started to wag its tail. Then it leaned forward and licked him on the hand. Eurylochus didn't even have time to think of using his spear.

At that moment, the singing stopped. The front door opened and a lovely woman emerged.

"Do not fear the beasts, stranger. They are my creatures. They protect me, and I protect them. Would you and your men like to come in for a meal?"

After a moment's pause, the men raced for the door. Eurylochus was trampled in their rush. He tried to convince them not to go in, but to no **avail**.

Eurylochus swore under his breath. "Fools!" he muttered. "Something's wrong here. Who ever heard of tame lions and wolves? Just catch me going into that house! Or letting go of this sword." He waved the weapon **defiantly** in the air.

Outside the door, Eurylochus waited and listened. At first all seemed well. He heard his men laughing and singing.

Suddenly their voices died down. He heard a few shouts and then horrible squeals.

Eurylochus' heart leapt. What was happening to his men?

For a moment, Eurylochus hesitated. Then fear seized him and he turned and ran. Straight back to Odysseus he flew.

By the time Eurylochus reached the ship, he was **hysterical**. "Odysseus! She's killed them! She's eaten them! She's done something horrible to them!"

"She who? Who's this she? Slow down. Someone get this fellow a cup of wine!" Odysseus commanded.

Eurylochus wailed even louder. "A woman! I don't know her name! My men went into the house. I heard them laughing and eating. Then came these horrible squeals! It was awful—inhuman! So I ran back here!"

At once Odysseus picked up his sword and spear. "Take me to the house, Eurylochus!"

"Me? Why me?"

"Stay then!" Odysseus shouted, too worried to argue.

"Shall we come with you, Odysseus?" one of his men yelled at his back.

Odysseus didn't even turn or slow down. "No! I won't lose another man under my command!"

With his hunter's eyes, Odysseus was able to track Eurylochus' trail. He found the house without trouble. It looked as calm and pleasant as ever. Eurylochus' tale seemed just a nightmare. Still, Odysseus knew all too well that many things are not what they seem.

Odysseus was just about to step into the clearing when a young man appeared. Odysseus stepped back and raised his spear.

The stranger held up his hand. "Have no fear of me, Odysseus. The gods have sent me to your aid."

"Hermes?"[8] Odysseus questioned. The young man bowed in **acknowledgment**.

"Now, where do you think you're going, Odysseus?" the god asked with a smile. "Are you still wandering into places you know nothing about?"

"My men are in that house!" Odysseus answered. "I'm not leaving without them!"

"Do you know who lives there? Well, I'll tell you. Her name is Circe,[9] and she's a goddess as well as a witch. But I warn you, she's no friend to humans.

"I'll also tell you what she's done to your men. It's a trick that she favors. She likes to invite passing strangers to feast on drugged food. Then she touches them with her magic wand, turning them into the animals of her choice. I'm afraid she elected to make your men pigs. They're in her **sty** right now, digging in the mud."

"Witch!" Odysseus angrily hissed. "Let her try any of her spells on me and she'll regret it."

"Ah, but Odysseus, she's a clever woman," warned Hermes. "See those lions and wolves prowling about her yard? They are more unlucky men who walked through Circe's front door. And the same thing will happen to you. Unless you eat this."

Hermes held out a white flower with a black stem.

"What is it?" Odysseus asked as he took the flower.

"It's called moly.[10] It will protect you from her drugs and that magic wand."

Odysseus nodded and ate the flower while Hermes continued. "Here's what you must do. Eat her food and drink her wine. Then, when she reaches for her wand, draw your sword. Rush toward her as if you might kill her. She will **cower** and ask for mercy. Make her swear that she'll practice no more magic on you or your men. Make her swear it by the gods." With those wise words, Hermes disappeared.

---

[8](her′ mēz) Hermes was the messenger god.
[9](sir′ sē)
[10](mō lē)

Odysseus took one more look around and then headed into the clearing. Again, the lions and wolves did not try to attack. They simply twitched their tails and watched him.

Odysseus stopped just outside Circe's house. Quick as a cat, the lovely witch was at the door. She eagerly invited Odysseus in and offered him food and drink.

The image of the animals outside haunted Odysseus. Nevertheless, he bravely ate the meal.

After Odysseus finished, Circe gave a wicked smile. Then she reached for her magic wand and tapped him.

At once Odysseus leapt up. In a moment, he had his sword **poised** at her throat.

Circe sank to her knees. "Who are you?" she cried. "How can you resist my magic? No other man has done that."

Suddenly a light of understanding crossed her face. "Odysseus? Are you Odysseus, the man the gods said would visit me?"

"I am he," answered Odysseus. "And did the gods also tell you that I'd kill you? For I will, witch. That is, unless you swear you'll cast no more spells on me or my men."

Circe grew pale indeed. "I swear by the River Styx in the black kingdom of Hades.[11] You know that no god will break such an oath. I swear I will not harm you."

Odysseus lowered his sword, and Circe sighed in relief. Then a smile spread across her face. "Now what about a true feast, Odysseus? Surely a man who has been so long at sea has a hearty appetite."

At once Circe prepared a huge meal. This time she used no magic drugs.

But Odysseus simply played with his food. He could think of nothing but his men.

"Why aren't you eating, Odysseus?" asked Circe.

"I cannot eat while my men are in that sty."

"Oh, is that all?" Circe opened the front door and disappeared.

[11] (stiks) (hā′ dēz) Hades is the kingdom of the Underworld, where dead soul stay. It is also the name of the god who rules that world.

Odysseus followed her out to the pigpen. He found Circe standing in the center of a dozen grunting pigs. She touched her wand to each of them.

Instantly, they became the men they used to be. They recognized Odysseus at once. With happy shouts and tears of joy, they rushed to thank him.

Circe was touched.

"Odysseus, my home is yours for as long as you wish. I know this journey has been long and **hazardous** for you and your men. If I can, I'd like to restore your spirits. Then when it's time to go, I'll send you off with advice the gods gave me."

Odysseus **conferred** with his men. In the end, they all agreed to stay.

"Good!" Circe exclaimed. "Now go to your ship and bring the others back here. We'll all have a feast to celebrate!"

Odysseus went back to the ship. When his men saw him, they gave happy shouts.

"Odysseus! You're back! You're safe! But what happened to the others?"

Odysseus briefly told the story. Then he concluded, "They're in the house of the goddess Circe. And having a wonderful time. You're invited to join them!"

"Join them doing what?" said Eurylochus, full of doubts.

"Laughing. Singing. Dancing. Eating. Making pigs of themselves. Are you familiar with such things, Eurylochus?" Odysseus asked jokingly.

The men were ready to go in minutes. But as they headed toward the forest, Eurylochus shouted after them.

"You fools! I can't believe you're going! Circe is a witch. What makes you think she hasn't put a spell on Odysseus? What makes you think this even *is* Odysseus? She can change men into animals. Maybe she can change chairs into men! Suppose this goddess just wants more pets to guard her house? Did you ever think of that?"

Eurylochus snorted. "Maybe you're foolish enough to go," he continued. "But I'm not! I remember the last time I followed Odysseus blindly. That day some of us ended up as a giant's dinner!"

Odysseus gripped his sword angrily. Then he got the better of his temper. "There comes a point, my friend, when caution is **lethal**. Just as lethal as being reckless. Trust to the gods, Eurylochus. And your own wits."

He turned and waved his men on. For a minute or more, Eurylochus stubbornly stood his ground. But after a nervous look around, he followed.

When the group arrived at Circe's house, they all had a huge feast. They danced and sang until the moon slipped off to bed.

Days passed and slid into months. In fact, a full year **elapsed** before any of them noticed. Every man was enjoying the peaceful island too much to grow restless. Even Eurylochus forgot to grumble.

But a day came when the men did grow homesick. Then they all agreed to sail for Ithaca as soon as possible.

Odysseus told Circe of their plans. "You have been kind and generous to us," he finished. "This year has healed my men. Once more they're fit for the sea. I owe you great thanks."

An **impish** smile rose to Circe's lips. "You have the memory of a king, Odysseus. You nobly forgive and forget." Odysseus smiled, too. He quite clearly recalled his first meeting with the goddess.

"I will miss you, dear Odysseus," Circe replied. "But I understand your longing for home."

She clasped his hands and then released them. "Now for the advice the gods gave me." The goddess revealed their words. Then with a final farewell, they parted.

Odysseus' crew prepared to set sail with all the energy of well-rested men. Yet they noticed Odysseus seemed a little distant. Some deep thoughts appeared to be **absorbing** his attention.

In good time, the ship set sail. And then the men turned eagerly to Odysseus. "Our course, Odysseus? Which direction are we heading?"

Odysseus stirred as if just awakened. "We go to speak to the prophet Teiresias.[12] He will tell us of the troubles ahead. With his help, we'll find our way home."

Most of the men cheered. But Eurylochus pushed forward, his face pale with fear.

"Teiresias, the blind **seer**? But, Odysseus, he's dead!"

Odysseus nodded thoughtfully. "So he is, Eurylochus. But the gods have told me he is the one to set us back on course. So by the heavens, I'll seek him out. Even though I must travel to the land of the dead to find him!"

[12](ti rē′ si as)

INSIGHTS

The blind Greek poet Homer supposedly wrote *The Odyssey,* from which this tale comes. No one knows if Homer really existed, let alone if he was blind. Scholars do guess that a final version of the myth appeared around the 8th century B.C.

Homer may be a myth. But Odysseus has seemed solid enough to fascinate us throughout the ages. Later Greeks saw him as a cruel, lying trickster. The Romans agreed that he was tricky but liked his persistence. In the Middle Ages, some saw him as a man on a deeply spiritual quest. Others thought he was a magician.

By the 15th century, Odysseus was the ideal man, a mix of scholar and knight. Then for the Victorians, he became a model of brave determination. Finally, in the 20th century, he turned into a symbol for every man.

So which is the real Odysseus?

Circe was one of the first witches in written history. (Medea, her niece, was another.) And from other tales about her, Odysseus was lucky to escape alive. She often used spells and magic drugs to get her way. She also killed her husband because she wasn't happy with her marriage.

Many legends state that Circe and Odysseus were lovers. This proved to be a fatal attraction. Odysseus was mistakenly killed by Telegonus, his son by Circe. Then Telegonus married Penelope, Odysseus' wife. And Circe married Telemachus, Odysseus' son by Penelope. The match had an unhappy end, however, for Telemachus killed Circe. It seems that along with loving epics, the Greeks liked a good soap opera, too.

In this story, Eurylochus wisely chose not to accept Circe's hospitality. But he wasn't as wise when they reached Sicily. There he stole Apollo's sacred cattle. As a result, the angry god saw that everyone but Odysseus was drowned.

Moly, the flower that protected Odysseus against Circe's spells, doesn't really exist. But certain types of garlic have been called moly. The reason? Because if you eat garlic, its odor will probably stop others from getting close enough to cast a spell.

Hermes, the messenger of the gods, had to travel very swiftly. For this reason, he wore wings on his cap and sandals. He was equipped with another symbol of his duty: a *caduceus,* or staff. Most messengers in ancient times carried a special staff so they would be recognized and treated well. But as suits a god, Hermes had a unique staff. It had wings on it as well.

AENEAS' TRIP TO THE UNDERWORLD

VOCABULARY PREVIEW

Below is a list of words that appear in the story. Read the list and get to know the words before you start the story.

adultery—sex between a married person and someone he or she is not married to; unfaithfulness
assured—freed from doubt
bough—tree limb or branch
collapsed—fell down or apart
condemned—wrongdoers; those judged guilty of crimes
descendants—offspring; children, great-grandchildren, etc.
desperately—in a wild, almost hopeless, way
destiny—one's future or fate
domain—area controlled by a ruler; kingdom
edict—an order or command
endured—put up with
ferries—carries people or things across a river or stream in a boat
fork—a split or division
predict—to say what the future will be; foretell
reincarnated—reborn in another body
sacrificed—killed a victim or gave a gift in order to honor a god
scowled—frowned
selflessness—unselfishness; generosity
slight—neglect; snub
unsheathe—draw (a sword) from its case; uncover

AENEAS'
TRIP
TO THE
UNDERWORLD

from *THE AENEID*

To find a home, sometimes you must travel farther than you ever dreamed — or dreaded.

Aeneas[1] woke in a sweat. Panting, crying, wanting his nightmare to have been a false dream.

But it wasn't. His nightmare had recaptured all the evils he had **endured** in the past years. The capture of Troy, his homeland, by the sneaky Greeks and their wooden horse was true.[2] The death of his wife was true.

[1] (ē nē′ as)

[2] (troi) The Greeks fought the Trojans for ten years to punish them for the theft of a Greek leader's wife. The Greeks won the war by building a huge wooden horse and hiding inside. Once the horse was pulled inside the city, the Greeks attacked.

And it was also true he had had a vision. It told him to flee his doomed city and find a new home for the gods and people of Troy.

After much fighting and dying, Aeneas did as he was told. He had led a group of his people, his aged father, and his young son safely out of the city. Then they had set sail to search for their new home.

Now Aeneas blinked in the darkness as he wiped away the tears. His mind raced through the past seven years of wandering. He and his people had anchored their ship many times and come ashore to build a new home.

But every time they tried, they failed. Many of the Trojans died from disease and starvation. Aeneas' father, Anchises,[3] had been among those.

Their ships had been set afire as well. Others were lost in violent storms and many Trojans drowned. Aeneas' pilot and friend Palinurus[4] was among those who had fallen overboard.

In the silence of the night, Aeneas prayed. Maybe the gods could help him find a new home for the future Trojan children.

Suddenly his father's ghost appeared by his bed. "Dear son," he said. "The great god Jupiter[5] has sent me to tell you to leave this place. Take only your bravest and strongest with you to Italy.

"Once you are in Italy, seek out the Sibyl,[6] who can **predict** the future. Ask her to lead you to the Underworld, the kingdom of Pluto.[7] You will find me there, among the blessed. I will answer your questions about your future. Farewell until then, my son."

The next morning, Aeneas told his people of Jupiter's command. He took only his strongest and bravest and set sail for Italy.

[3] (an kī′ sēz)
[4] (pal i nū′ rus)
[5] (jū′ pi ter) Jupiter was the chief god of the Romans.
[6] (sib′ il)
[7] (plū′ tō) Pluto was the god who ruled the dead.

As the rocky cliffs came within sight, Aeneas shouted orders. "Cast out the anchors! Prepare to go ashore!"

The Trojans leaped happily from their ships. They were eager to explore the new land. But Aeneas quickly went alone up the steep cliff to the Sibyl's cave.

The Sibyl was a very wise woman. She not only could see into the future. She also knew how to cross the bridge between life and death.

Aeneas walked bravely into the dark cave. A light led him into a huge room with a sandy floor. The ceiling towered overhead as high as a mountain.

Aeneas stopped and then spun around to look in all directions. He saw a hundred tunnels all leading to this one central room.

"Where is the light coming from?" he wondered.

Then he saw the Sibyl seated on a high rock waiting for him.

In a deep, echoing voice, she spoke. "It is good to see you, goddess-born Aeneas.[8] The light you were wondering about is the light given to you by the gods."

She paused and stared at him. Then she said, "I have heard much of your travels and your bravery. You lead the Trojans with **selflessness**, good faith, and wisdom. And your search will come to a happy end. You will find a homeland. But not without more wars, bloodshed, and suffering."

"I ask for no more than my **destiny**," replied Aeneas. "Yet I do need your help. The ghost of my father has asked me to meet him in the Underworld. I hope you will help me. The opening to Pluto's kingdom is near here, isn't it?"

"Aeneas, you may be able to enter the Underworld," the Sibyl said. "The gates are open day and night. But it is not so easy to escape the hands of death. Many have tried. But few have come back alive.

"Yet if you are determined to see your father," she continued, "I will go with you. First, however, you must bring

[8] Aeneas was the son of Venus (vē′ nus), the Roman goddess of love and beauty.

me a golden **bough**. That is the gift Proserpina,[9] Pluto's queen of the Underworld, likes so much. If you are meant to enter the gates of death, you will find the bough hidden in the forest. And you will easily be able to break it off from the tree trunk."

Immediately Aeneas set out to find the golden bough. As he entered the deep forest, he wondered how he would ever find a single bough among so many branches.

Suddenly Aeneas saw two doves. He knew at once that they belonged to his mother, Venus.

"Follow us, Aeneas," they sweetly chanted. "We will guide you to your golden bough."

They flew slowly enough so that Aeneas could follow. He soon realized they were leading him to Lake Avernus.[10] This was the water the Sibyl had told him was the mouth to the Underworld.

Finally the doves landed on a branch. Aeneas went up to the tree and pushed his hand among the branches.

A warm feeling came over him. When he withdrew his hand, the golden bough was in it. At once, the tree grew another bough in its place. It was just as golden as the last.

Aeneas hurriedly returned to the Sibyl's cave and gave her the bough. But she didn't want it.

"You keep it," she said. "You will need it if you intend to enter the land of the dead while still living."

Then she led Aeneas, along with four black cows, back to the edge of the foggy lake. She pointed out a cave across the water. Aeneas could barely see its huge mouth.

The Sibyl whispered in his ear. "No winged creature can fly across this lake. The fog rises like a big hand to pluck them from the sky. Therefore, we must ask the gods for help."

So together, they built an altar on the shore and set it afire. The flames shot to the heavens.

The Sibyl **sacrificed** the four cows. Pouring wine on their

[9](pro ser' pi na)
[10](a ver' nus)

heads, she cut the hair from between their horns. Then she laid the hair on the roaring fires. This was to be the first gift to Proserpina, the goddess of the dead.

Next, the Sibyl instructed Aeneas to put the dead animals upon the flames. Then she threw her arms into the air and prayed.

"Goddess of the Underworld! You who watch over the souls of the dead! Open the gates to your mysterious **domain** deep in the earth! Grant us passage into your world! And by your will, we shall move among the ghosts. We shall see what secrets are buried from the World of Light."

With that prayer spoken, the Sibyl and Aeneas poured boiling bull fat over the blazing animals. Then as they watched over the fire, Aeneas fell asleep.

At dawn, he was abruptly awakened. All around him trees were shaking and wild dogs howling. And the earth was roaring with the voice of ten thousand bulls.

Suddenly the goddess cried out from within the Sibyl's body. In the mighty voice of Proserpina, she spoke.

"Run, all who do not wish to enter the land of the dead! Run! Aeneas, **unsheathe** your sword and follow me! You will need courage!"

The Sibyl ran straight into the foggy lake and disappeared. Close behind her, Aeneas fearlessly followed.

To his surprise, Aeneas did not touch any water. Instead, he found himself inside the cave across the lake. He was miles under the earth and standing in front of the gates of Tartarus.[11] The Sibyl was at his side.

Aeneas stared in amazement and horror at the sights. All around him danced the ghostly evils of the world. He saw Disease, Old Age, Grief, Fear, Starvation, Death, Pain, and War.

Quickly Aeneas and the Sibyl passed through the gates. But there they only found more horrors. This time terrible

---

[11] (tar' tar us) Many Roman poets used this name as another way to refer to the Underworld.

monsters surrounded them. There were Centaurs[12] —half-human, half-horse beings. A nine-headed snake. A three-bodied giant. A hundred-handed giant. A fire-breathing fish.

Medusa,[13] the girl with hair made of serpents, was there, too. Any person who looked at her would be turned into stone.

Suddenly a bird-woman swooped right in front of Aeneas. He lifted his sword to kill her, but the Sibyl grabbed his sword.

"You are in the Underworld, Aeneas," she said. "These monsters are only ghosts of what they once were. You cannot kill them, and they cannot kill you."

Despite the Sibyl's words, Aeneas was glad to leave the monsters behind. They continued walking until they stood on the banks of a river. Its water swirled into thick, muddy pools.

As Aeneas stared across the water, he saw an old man rowing a boat toward them. The man's eyes were flames of fire. His chin was covered with a mass of straggly hair. And his ragged clothes looked greased to his skin.

"Who is that?" Aeneas asked.

"That is Charon.[14] He **ferries** the dead across the river. Watch," answered the Sibyl.

Sure enough, as Charon's boat touched shore, ghosts appeared and rushed toward him. The ghosts were males and females of every size and age. In a pitiful way, they stretched out their hands, begging to be taken aboard. But the gloomy ferryman carefully chose his passengers. He took some and pushed others away.

Aeneas turned to the Sibyl. "Where do these ghosts want to go? Why did Charon choose that woman and reject that little boy?"

"Those he turns away are the unburied dead," replied the Sibyl. "The bank across this river is the entrance to

[12](sen' torz)
[13](me dū' sa)
[14](ka' ron)

Pluto's kingdom. Charon cannot take them across until they have been given a proper funeral.''

"Do you mean they will remain here forever if Charon wishes?'' worried Aeneas.

"It is not Charon's **edict**, but Pluto's. Only after they have wandered on these banks for a hundred years can Charon take them across. Now, let us see him ourselves,'' the Sibyl said.

As they neared the boat, Aeneas stopped in astonishment. Ahead of him he saw his trusty pilot who had drowned in the last storm.

"Palinurus! I have missed you, my friend,'' Aeneas cried happily.

"I have missed you too, my prince—you who led us to safety,'' answered Palinurus.

Aeneas hung his head. "I did not lead you to safety.''

"Ah, Aeneas, that was not your fault. A rough wave knocked me into the sea. I took the rudder[15] with me in my fall. And I chose to cling to it, rather than try to return to the ship.''

Palinurus shut his eyes at the pain of the memory. Then he said, "I would ask you a favor, however. Take me across the river with you. Charon will not let me pass.''

The Sibyl spoke up at once. "You know better than to change the laws of Pluto! Go on your way, Palinurus, and let us go on ours!''

Palinurus **desperately** begged, "Then find my body, dear prince! Throw handfuls of dirt on it so that my spirit may have rest! Please!''

The Sibyl spoke again but in a softer voice. "Your time will soon come, Palinurus. Your body will be found by a coastal people. And they will give you a proper funeral. They will even name the farthest most rock after you.''

With that, the ghost of Palinurus vanished.

---

[15] The rudder is a wood or metal piece attached to the rear of a boat. It helps steer the boat.

The Sibyl turned to the bank once again and led Aeneas to Charon. When the ferryman caught sight of Aeneas, he drew back.

"Who are you?" he demanded. His voice echoed through the rocky canyon. "Who, living and bearing arms, dares walk the land of Shadows, Sleep, and Night? Tell me your purpose."

He **scowled** and then declared, "I may not ferry the living across this river in my boat. I took a few only because their fathers were gods. But they caused great mischief. One tried to carry off Cerberus,[16] Pluto's three-headed dog. And the other two tried to steal Pluto's queen."[17]

The Sibyl **assured** him. "Do not fear us. We are not here to make mischief. Aeneas, the goddess-born Trojan, is famous for his honor, courage, and skill in war. He must see his father. If I cannot convince you to take us across, this surely will."

Without another word, the Sibyl held up Aeneas' arm. Even in the dim light of the Underworld, the golden bough gleamed.

Instantly Charon chased the ghosts away and helped the two on board. The boat groaned under Aeneas' weight. Charon's usual ghostly passengers weighed nothing at all. Yet the boat managed to carry them safely to the opposite shore.

As Aeneas climbed the bank, an awful howl arose. He stopped and stared at the fearsome creature in his path. "Cerberus," he whispered. The savage dog threw back all its three heads and howled once more.

Aeneas drew his sword and stepped forward. This beast was surely no ghost. So if there was no other way past, he would have to kill the monster.

But the Sibyl called, "Aeneas, sheathe your sword. It will not be needed."

[16] (ser' ber us)
[17] Charon is referring to Heracles, Theseus, and Peirithous.

With that she took out a cake from a bag she carried and tossed it to the dog. The greedy Cerberus swallowed the cake. Then almost immediately the huge dog **collapsed**.

"Dead?" asked Aeneas.

The Sibyl shook her head. "Merely sleeping. The cake contained a drug."

Aeneas and his guide walked on into the gloom. In a low voice, the Sibyl announced, "We have reached the kingdom of Pluto."

As they stepped into that dark region, a terrible, lonely sound rose around them. It was the cries of babies torn from life just after birth.

Aeneas covered his ears. He could not bear their sad cries.

"You must remain strong," the Sibyl reminded him.

Next were the ghosts of the suicides, the victims of unhappy love. Aeneas cried out when he saw Dido, the queen of Carthage.[18] Tears sprang into his eyes as he spoke.

"Poor Dido! The rumor was true then. You did take your own life! Was I the cause, dear Dido? I swear I did not want to leave you! The gods can tell you I was only following their wishes, not my own! Will you forgive me?"

Dido kept her eyes on the ground. She did not seem to hear or see him. Finally she turned and walked away. Aeneas followed her, still pleading for forgiveness. But Dido kept walking.

Aeneas finally stopped and sat down. He wiped the tears from his eyes and cheeks. What he had been forced to do was in the past. Now he must find his father for the sake of the Trojan people.

Farther down the road, Aeneas and the Sibyl came upon the ghosts of war heroes. Aeneas' Trojan friends greeted him warmly. They asked many questions and were eager to talk over old times. But when his old enemies—the Greeks—saw Aeneas and his sword, they fled.

---

[18](dī' do) (kar' thij) Dido fell in love with Aeneas when he stopped in her kingdom. After he left, she killed herself in despair.

Aeneas wanted to stay with his Trojan friends. But the Sibyl insisted they go on. "You cannot waste time joking with old friends. Come."

The Sibyl guided him onward until they reached a **fork** in the road. There they stopped.

"Where do these roads lead?" asked Aeneas.

"To the right are the Elysian[19] Fields where you will find your father," the Sibyl answered. "To the left are the **condemned**."

"Who are the condemned? What have they done?" Aeneas felt pity for them.

"They are sinners who are being punished in death for crimes they committed in life. Even if I had a hundred tongues, I could not tell you all their crimes or all their punishments. There are those who hated their relatives or killed a parent. Some refused to share their money. Still others committed **adultery** or fought in civil wars."

She continued, "At the bottom of the pit lies a giant. His body covers nine acres. Vultures feast on his liver. But just as fast as it is eaten, the liver grows again. His punishment has no end.

"Another must roll a huge boulder up a steep hill. But at the top, the rock tumbles down again. So he must roll the boulder back up the hill over and over again.

"Another is condemned to endlessly shout, 'I warn you to be fair. Do not **slight** the gods.' "

The Sibyl took his arm. "But come, Aeneas. Let us find your father. The arched gates are before us."

However, Aeneas could not enter the gates until he had honored Proserpina. So he bent on his knee and planted the golden bough in the soft soil. Then the Sibyl sprinkled water on his body, and they passed through the gate.

After all the horrors of the Underworld, Aeneas was not prepared for this place. He couldn't believe the beauty he saw. In front of him stretched grassy meadows and rows

[19](e lizh' i an)

of fruit trees. A soft purple light bathed the fields, and sweet music filled the air. Aeneas felt instantly at peace.

And the people! Everywhere he looked, Aeneas saw the ghosts of those who had helped others. Over there were all the greatest heroes of the Trojan War. They now sat in small groups listening to music. Their horses, set free, roamed nearby.

Aeneas also noticed priests, who were dancing and singing in happy voices. He saw, too, some famous poets gathered nearby. The Sibyl asked this group where they might find Anchises.

But as soon as they asked, a man rushed toward them. "At last you have come!" he cried out.

It was Anchises, Aeneas' father. He reached his arms out toward his son. "I've been worried about you, dear son. But I knew that your love and courage would see you past all dangers."

"Your ghost, Father, came to me and kept me on the right path. I'm deeply grateful. Now let me embrace you!"

Aeneas tried to hug his father, but his hands simply passed through the air. His father seemed so real. It was hard to remember that Anchises was a ghost.

Aeneas had to be content with just words. "I have missed you, Father," he said. "Yet I shall now be able to think of you in this happy place. But tell me, Father, what of my people? What of the Trojans still alive? What of our future?"

Anchises gestured at all the famous souls. "This is your future, my son. All these noble souls are here waiting for their second bodies. When they have been here 1,000 years, they drink from this river and forget their past. Then they return to the world and are **reincarnated**."

Anchises smiled proudly. "I have wanted to show them to you for so long. They are the future of your race. No longer can you doubt your destiny in Italy."

Anchises led his son to a hill overlooking a valley of souls waiting to go to earth. Here, he pointed out Aeneas' future son, grandson, and other **descendants**.

"See the glory your Trojan line will achieve? Your Italian children will raise your name to the very stars and beyond! Your destiny, my son, is to govern the people of the world with order. To make peace a habit. To spare the beaten. And to crush the proud."

Aeneas stared long and hard at his father. "Thank you, dear Father. You have restored my hope for the future of our Trojan race. I will serve you and all of them."

Anchises smiled. Then he led his son and the Sibyl to the Gates of Sleep. "Farewell, my son."

"Farewell, Father."

Aeneas and the Sibyl quickly made their way back to the earth. After thanking the Sibyl, Aeneas raced to his ships. He happily greeted his fellow Trojans. Then at the top of his lungs he shouted: "Set sail, my people! We are off to find our promised home!"

INSIGHTS

Virgil, author of *The Aeneid,* was viewed as the greatest poet of ancient Rome. And *The Aeneid* was regarded as Rome's national epic—a beautiful mix of myth, history, and poetry. Yet Virgil turned poet only because he felt too shy to become a lawyer.

The fame he earned should have convinced Virgil of his talent. However, he left orders upon his death that the poem he was still working on should be destroyed. Though he'd spent ten years on the poem, he felt it wasn't worth publishing.

But the future emperor, Augustus, knew the value of the poet's work. Not only did he see that it was saved. He also ordered two of Virgil's friends to finish the epic. Thus *The Aeneid* came safely into the world after all.

A poem that doubles as a reference? It seems unlikely. However, the Romans greatly admired Virgil's poems about shepherds and farming. In fact, they used them as texts in their schools.

The Romans weren't the only ones who respected Virgil. English writers in particular, including Wordsworth and Tennyson, were also influenced by Virgil. Dryden, another poet, translated *The Aeneid* into English. Milton paid an equally grand compliment by imitating Virgil in *Paradise Lost.*

The great Italian poet Dante went one step further. He not only imitated Virgil. He included the Roman poet as a character in his epic poem *The Divine Comedy.*

continued

Aeneas was a powerful figure for the Romans. Great families often boasted he was their ancestor. In fact, they even thought of him as a god. They called him *Jupiter indiges* ("Jupiter, god of the nation") after their chief god.

The custom of claiming Aeneas as an ancestor even spread to other lands. In Elizabethan times, some Britons still said that their country had been settled by an ancestor of Aeneas.

The Sibyl visited by Aeneas was a creature both gifted and cursed. The god Apollo granted her the power to foretell the future.

The Sibyl also asked for everlasting youth. But Apollo was annoyed with her for refusing to be his mistress. Therefore, he granted her only one year for each grain of sand she could hold in her hand. This totaled 1,000 years. (She was 700 years old when she helped Aeneas.)

But even that gift of 1,000 years was not joyful. For Apollo commanded that each year, the Sibyl would shrink a little more. Finally nothing was left but her voice.

THE FOLLIES OF MIDAS

VOCABULARY PREVIEW

Below is a list of words that appear in the story. Read the list and get to know the words before you start the story.

adorned—decorated
chambers—rooms, especially bedrooms
confiding—telling in secret
deliriously—wildly; madly
duo—pair
enraptured—delighted; thrilled
foster—acting as a relative; adoptive
goblet—wine glass
gracious—kind; polite
guffaws—loud laughs; roars of laughter
inadequate—unsatisfactory; not enough
nudged—pushed or elbowed
obsessed—absorbed and fascinated by
plight—difficult situation
procession—moving line of people or things; parade
renounce—give up
retorted—replied cleverly or sharply
revelry—merrymaking; celebration
tutor—private teacher
verdict—decision; judgment

The
FOLLIES
of MIDAS

Can a man be too rich or too honest for his own good? King Midas certainly didn't think so. But even an uncommon fool like Midas can be forced to see the error of his ways — if the gods are the teachers.

A song rang big and bold throughout the forest.

I'm lost! Oh, I'm lost!
But I'm having a wonderful time!
I have plenty of lovely women
And plenty of fine, old wine!

Over and over the song was repeated. It grew louder and then slurred. Now the singer warbled in a high voice. Then he bellowed in a low voice.

Finally the singer bounded out of the trees. And a strange sight he was. A man from his waist up—apart from his ears and horns. A goat from his waist down. But then all satyrs[1] looked like that.

[1] (sā′ terz or sat′ erz)

This satyr was named Silenus,[2] and he was feeling very merry. He skipped to the rhythm of his tune. Dust and rocks flew in all directions.

From their place in the trees, birds and squirrels scolded him. "Do you have to send clouds of dust our way?" they complained. "Stop it, Silenus! You're filling our nests with dirt!"

A song was their only reply.

> *Natter! Chatter! Patter!*
> *I'm not listening to you!*
> *I'll sing and romp the way I like*
> *Until the moon's gone blue!*

Onward Silenus pranced, still singing and dancing. Now and again he paused for breath and another mouthful of wine.

Farther down the road, Silenus finally stopped. Hadn't he been looking for someone? Ah, yes. His favorite pupil and **foster** son, Bacchus.[3] And his fellow satyrs.

But where were they? He'd thought they were in these woods. Or were they in the woods to the north?

Silenus couldn't remember. Maybe he'd even passed them by without seeing them. His eyesight wasn't what it used to be.

Silenus sat down with his back against an oak tree. He'd rest for only a moment or two. Maybe Bacchus would find him if he stayed in one place.

"So nice here under this tree," Silenus muttered drowsily. His head drooped. Soon heavy snores could be heard.

The wood remained quiet for several hours. But then came some new visitors . . . .

"Shh, shh. You'll wake him."

"Is he alive or dead?"

"He smells like a wine cellar!"

[2](sī lē′ nus)
[3](bak′ kus)

"What kind of man is this? He has the horns, ears, and legs of a goat!"

"Wait 'til our King Midas[4] sees this!"

The men who surrounded Silenus were servants of Midas. They had been sent out to collect roses for the king. But the sight of the satyr had made them forget their chore.

The tallest of the men **nudged** the smallest. "Wake him up!"

The smaller replied with a stronger nudge. "You wake him!"

The taller nearly knocked him to the ground. "No! You do it!"

The smaller instantly recovered and was ready to strike back. But another man stepped between them.

"Stop that nonsense, you two! No one needs to wake him up at all. As if we could when he's dead drunk! Now go fetch those roses and get back here. I've a plan in mind."

The other two did as they were told. Soon they were on their return trip home to Midas' palace. Silenus was with them, still asleep. They'd draped him over the back of an ass.

As this small **procession** moved down the road, peasants in the fields stared. Some crowded closer to see the odd creature.

"What do you have on the back of that ass?" one peasant shouted.

The taller servant yelled back, "Your wife, dear sir! Picked her up on the road this morning! A hairy little thing, ain't she?"

As you might imagine, the peasant found the joke mildly insulting. He chased the servants with a shower of well-aimed rocks.

The rocks helped speed the servants on their way. Soon they reached the palace. They found their king waiting for them, wondering about their delay.

[4](mī′ das)

"King Midas!" they cried. "Look at this beggar we found in your wood! Surely removing him from your kingdom deserves some reward?"

Midas stared at the satyr. Then he ordered, "Get him off that ass and bring him here."

Two of the servants quickly brought old Silenus to Midas. The satyr was **adorned** from head to toe with wreaths of roses.

King Midas stared once more. At last he said, "Here's your reward then. Bring me a jug of wine, a plate of meat, and a loaf of bread."

The servants started to lead Silenus off. However, a new order stopped them. "No, leave him here!"

"But King—"

"Do as I bid!"

The servants hurried down the hallway to the kitchen. When they returned with the food, they found Silenus sitting at the table. He and Midas were laughing and joking. No one would guess they weren't old friends.

The servants stopped short in surprise. Mouths and jaws dropped as they watched the odd scene.

Midas and Silenus took one look at them and burst out laughing. "You fools," Midas said. "You all look as stupid as they say *I* am!"

The king gestured at the Satyr. "The gentleman before you is Silenus. He is foster father and **tutor** of Bacchus." Midas noted their startled glances. "Yes, I said Bacchus. It seems even you fools know the god of wine and **revelry**."

Silenus nodded happily at this information.

Midas continued, "Silenus has lost his way. We will return him to Bacchus. That is, after we do a little reveling of our own." Midas clapped his hands and the servants jumped. "Now serve this good fellow anything he wishes. Close your mouths and move!"

The servants speedily obeyed. Old Silenus drank heavily of the wine they served. And he emptied his plate just as fast as he drained his cup.

For ten days this feasting carried on. Midas and Silenus grew fat with food and drunk with wine. All that drinking made them a little lively. By the end of the first day, every plate in the palace had been broken.

Midas and Silenus didn't care about the trouble they caused. Silenus had the servants dress up in roses and dance around rose hoops. He and Midas laughed for hours at that.

But finally Midas realized Bacchus might be growing concerned. So he gathered his wits and set off with Silenus to find Bacchus.

The tottering **duo** soon found the god of wine. He gave the two a warm greeting. The sight of the satyr especially pleased him.

"My friend! Where have you been?" the god cried. "I thought you were lost for good this time!"

Bacchus gave Silenus a hug. "You old devil. Did you give Midas a difficult time?"

He didn't wait for an answer but turned to Midas. "Midas, I thank you. You deserve a gift for returning my teacher to me. Ask whatever you will, and I shall grant it."

Midas smiled secretly. He had known all along the god would offer some sort of reward for Silenus. Now the moment had come.

"Bacchus, you are far too **gracious**. But if you insist . . ."

Bacchus nodded.

"Then I wish that everything I touch will turn to gold."

Bacchus could scarcely believe such a greedy request. Midas was already the richest ruler in the land. Now he wanted more.

But Bacchus had offered. So he had to fulfill his promise.

"Very well, Midas. Your wish is granted. But in the future, I hope you pick your wishes more carefully."

A wiser man might have paused at those words. Not Midas. He went off **deliriously** happy.

Midas began trying out his power at once. He plucked a leaf from a tree. In an instant, it became a sunny gold!

He smiled broadly. "Ah, I'll paint a golden world for myself! Gold in gold upon gold I shall have."

When Midas reached the palace, he quickly gathered his servants. "Listen, I want a feast tonight. A huge feast! Invite all my neighbors as the guests!"

As Midas walked to his **chambers**, he thought over his plans. "This feast will finally convince people of my generosity. And they'll all wish they had my riches. Maybe this will stop them from calling me stupid."

That evening fifty guests were seated round the king's table. They stared at the golden vases filled with golden flowers. They listened to a musician pluck a golden lyre.[5] And they passed golden pitchers of wine.

After giving his guests time to look and wonder, Midas made his entrance. He stood at the head of the table and poured a **goblet** of wine. Then raising it, he said, "To your health, my good guests! I bid you welcome to my palace. May you enjoy the feast I've planned for you."

Midas sat down and brought the now-golden goblet to his lips. But when the wine hit his tongue, it turned to liquid gold.

Midas spat out the mouthful he had taken. "What's this?" he muttered. "Surely not *everything* I touch will turn to gold!"

He raised a chunk of bread to his mouth and bit down. But the bread, too, changed to gold. The same thing happened with a piece of meat he reached for.

Midas glared at his guests. They were all happily eating and drinking. Not one had noticed the foolish king's **plight**.

Midas' anger exploded. "I'm glad you're all enjoying yourselves!" he shouted. But you might like to know that I haven't been able to eat a bite! Everything I touch turns to gold! I may starve to death!"

The amused guests stared at the helpless, greedy king. They tried not to laugh, but some **guffaws** escaped.

---

[5] A lyre is a stringed instrument similar to a harp.

A few took pity on the king. They tried to feed him from their own plates. But again the food turned to gold when it touched Midas' lips.

The distressed king quickly left the table and went to his chambers. However, he found no peace there and certainly no sleep on his golden bed. Over and over he prayed the curse would be lifted by dawn.

The next day seemed to promise better things. The birds trilled carefree songs. The sun beamed over a bright blue sky. And a warm breeze gently batted the trees.

Midas eagerly ordered his breakfast set out in the garden. He almost trotted to the table. Hardly had he sat down before he dove into the food. However, nothing had changed. Every bit of food and every sip of wine turned to gold.

Midas sat back in his chair, defeated. He looked from his plate to his chair to his food. All gold.

"What good is gold if I can't eat or drink?" Midas complained. "At this rate, I won't be only the richest man in the world. I'll be the thinnest! By the gods, I'd rather be a poor man with a full belly."

Midas' stomach rumbled noisily. There was only one thing left to do. At once he set off to find Bacchus.

The god was not hard to find. Indeed, he seemed to be waiting for Midas.

"You look pale and weak, my friend," Bacchus commented. "What's the matter?"

"Your gift is the matter!" Midas **retorted**. "You knew I'd be unable to eat! Why did you grant my wish?"

"I gave you what you asked for, Midas. It's not my fault that your greed led you to forget simpler pleasures."

"You could have warned me."

"Would you have listened?" Bacchus asked. "No, the hard lessons must be experienced, not taught. They are for each of us to learn alone. But if you would like to **renounce** your wish, I can help you."

"Ah, good Bacchus, if you only would," Midas said.

"Very well. Go to the River Pactolus[6] and stand under its waterfall. The water will wash the wish from your body."

Relief rushed over Midas. "Great Bacchus, thank you. I'll never be so stupid again."

Midas was off in a flash. At the bank of the Pactolus, Midas dove into the huge pool. He came up under the waterfall and let the clear water flood over him. As it streamed down his body, it turned to liquid gold. Soon the whole river shimmered with golden water and sand.

Midas finished his bath and hurried back to the palace. He flew to the kitchen and grabbed some food. Without pausing for breath, he stuffed his mouth and chewed.

Ah! As Bacchus had promised, food was food once again. And it had never tasted so good.

The episode did seem to teach Midas a lesson. He became less **obsessed** with riches. The simple pleasures that Bacchus had spoken of grew more important to him.

But while Midas' greed had lessened, he hadn't been cured of stupidity. So Midas soon found himself in trouble again.

This next incident occurred as Midas was strolling through the woods one day. Suddenly a few sweet notes of music drifted to him. Midas was **enraptured**.

"How lovely!" Midas murmured. "But who can the musician be?"

Midas hurried in the direction of the music and came across the player. Or rather players, for there turned out to be two. And what players! The gods Pan and Apollo were the musicians.[7]

Midas hid behind a bush, eager to hear more music. He saw Pan gesturing at Apollo's jeweled lyre.

"Yes, your instrument is certainly a pretty thing," admitted Pan. "But so is the peacock. And he sings with all the appeal of a Harpy."[8]

[6] (pak tō' lus)

[7] (pan) (a pol' lō) Pan — half-goat, half-man — was a god of the forest. Apollo was the god of truth, light, and music.

[8] (har' pē) A Harpy is a monster with a young woman's head, a bird's body, and clawed feet.

Apollo frowned. But Pan didn't give the god a chance to reply. "I'd take my old pipe any day. It has the strength and sweetness of mountain water."

"Ah, well, I've always preferred wine," Apollo said. "But let's put the argument to the test. I propose a contest."

"Your lyre against my pipes?" Pan asked. "But who is to serve as judge?"

Apollo gestured towards the bush where Midas was hiding. "Why, Midas, of course."

Midas, embarrassed to have been discovered, slowly stood up. "Great gods, I did not mean to spy—"

"It's not your eyes we're interested in," Pan interrupted. "It's your ears we require. Now open them and listen."

Pan played first. His pipes rang out, strong and strangely haunting. To Midas, the song seemed as rough and beautiful as a wild mountain stream.

When the god finished, Apollo nodded. Then, with a moment's pause, he took up his lyre and played.

The god of music was a master of his instrument. The sounds flowed from his lyre like clouds on a spring breeze. Each note flowered and burst with the beauty of rosebuds. Even the birds and trees leaned forward to better hear the song.

When Apollo ended his music, he first turned to Pan. He found the god sitting with his eyes closed, a smile on his face.

Satisfied, Apollo turned to Midas. "Well, Midas? Your **verdict**?"

Midas bowed to both gods. Then clearing his throat, he said, "The verdict is obvious, mighty gods. Pan is the winner."

Pan's eyes popped open. He joined Apollo in staring at the king.

Apollo spoke for both of them. "So, you think Pan is the better player?"

"Yes, I do," said Midas firmly.

A gleam came into Apollo's eyes. Any smarter human would have taken one look and run. "Well, well, little king. I'm forced to accept your decision. But I should have guessed that with those ears, you might not be the best judge. Such tiny, **inadequate** ears. Really not quite up to the task. Now suppose I gave you—"

Apollo gestured at Midas. The king darted back, but too late. He felt a tickling at the side of his head. Suddenly he found his ears growing straight upward. Up and up they shot, until they were about a foot long. Then they sprouted fur. When Apollo was through, Midas had the ears of an ass.

Apollo laughed. "Now you have ears fit for a king. The King of Fools, that is."

The god laughed again. And this time Pan and the whole forest joined with him.

His face burning, Midas turned and fled back to his palace. He didn't stop running until he had locked his chamber doors behind him.

For days Midas refused to come out of his room. His food he took from trays left at his door. But for company, he had only his mirror.

Midas at last came up with the idea of wrapping his ears in a turban.[9] Though everyone stared at this strange fashion, Midas kept his secret. In fact, the only one who knew of Midas' plight was his barber. And Midas swore him to silence.

Yet after a time, the amazing secret began to weigh on the barber. It was like an itch he was desperate to scratch. But he knew if he told anyone, he'd pay with his life.

Finally one night, the barber could stand it no longer. He went to the riverbank and dug a small hole.

Then leaning down, the barber put his mouth in the hole. "Midas has ass' ears! Midas has ass' ears!" he whispered.

After **confiding** the secret, the barber felt better at once. He filled in the hole and went back to the palace.

---

[9] A turban is a hatlike scarf worn wrapped around the head.

A season passed and spring came. In the spot where the barber had whispered his secret, reeds sprouted. And as they grew, they swayed and passed the secret to the wind.

"Midas has ass' ears! Midas has ass' ears!"

The wind loved gossip. So it picked up the secret. To every tree, brook, bird, and human, it carried the news. Before too long, the whole kingdom had heard the voices on the wind. The peasants began to whisper among themselves.

"Did you hear that the king has ass' ears?"

"Have you heard that the king wears a turban to cover his ass' ears?"

At last Midas himself heard the whisper from the winds. And when he saw the strange glances from his servants, he knew the secret was out. The final blow came when he overheard two neighbors talking. "Well, if the rumor is true, it's only fitting. At last Midas looks like the ass he always was."

Silly Midas took the only revenge he could. He ordered the barber to be executed. Naturally the man heard the rumors on the gossiping wind and fled.

So Midas sat in his turban and let his hair grow long. He was and would always be the laughingstock of Greece.

INSIGHTS

According to one myth, Midas finally got rid of his ass' ears. Though he first planned revenge against his barber, Midas rethought the matter. He decided that since his greed was forgiven, the barber should be forgiven, too. Apollo approved of Midas' mercy and returned the king's ears to normal.

Another version doesn't end happily at all. This myth relates that Midas was so ashamed, he killed himself by drinking the blood of a bull.

Early Christians thought Pan was an evil creature. In fact, he came to be linked to the devil. That is why the Christian devil is often shown with horns, hooves, and tail.

Pan was also a symbol of the old Greek religion. Legend says that when Christ was killed, a voice boomed over the sea, "Great Pan is dead!" Thus the Olympians died as Christianity was born.

There are enough tales about Pan's affairs to back up the Christian view of him. But he was more than just a lover of women, as this story proves.

One day in the woods, Pan spotted lovely Syrinx. At once he fell in love with her. But this nymph wanted to remain pure. Therefore, she rejected Pan and fled. And Pan set off in pursuit.

Just as Pan was about to seize Syrinx, her sister nymphs came to the rescue. They changed Syrinx into a bed of reeds.

Pan gazed sadly at his lost love. As he did so, he heard a lovely sound. He realized that it was the wind blowing through the reeds.

Pan was inspired. He cut two of the reeds and glued them together with beeswax. And that was the origin of the Pan pipes.

There's a story behind Apollo's lyre, as well. The day he was born, playful Hermes stole Apollo's cattle. When the theft was discovered, Hermes calmed the angry Apollo by giving him a gift: the first lyre. Clever Hermes invented the instrument by stretching strings across a tortoise shell.

The gift delighted Apollo. The two gods became great friends, and Apollo turned into a master musician.

Myths can sometimes serve as a way for people to comment on their own lives. At least, the musician Bach found that to be true. In his musical version of this myth, he intended the tin-eared Midas to represent one of his critics.

In Greek myth, the satyrs are usually busy drinking or chasing women. Yet they had a more useful side, as well. They helped the great smith of the gods, Hephaestus, in his workshop.

In addition, the satyrs helped educate Bacchus. As hearty drinkers themselves, they had much in common with the god of wine.

That drinking wasn't always carefree. One story states that the satyrs were originally men. Because they neglected to watch over their pupil one day, Hera changed them into monkeys. (If you look at a picture of the satrys, you'll see both goatish and monkeylike traits.)

CUPID AND PSYCHE

VOCABULARY PREVIEW

Below is a list of words that appear in the story. Read the list and get to know the words before you start the story.

abyss—deep pit or canyon
adulation—extreme praise or respect
assaulted—attacked
bemused—confused; puzzled
broached—introduced; presented
brooding—worrying; thinking deeply
browse—feed; graze
conviction—strong belief
disfavor—disapproval
efficiency—ability to be quick and useful
embedded—firmly fixed into a surface
homage—public honor or praise
illuminated—lighted
imperious—bossy
mourning—grieving
somber—gloomy; dark
stupor—daze; trance
throng—crowd; mob
ushered—led; guided
wavered—trembled; flickered

Cupid
and Psyche

The odds are against the two
lovers in this story.
Jealous family members
and different backgrounds
threaten their frail relationship.
Yet in this case, the strength
of a human woman proves more
than a match for even
the gods.

In ancient times in Greece lived one of the most beautiful of all women: Psyche.[1] This maiden was so lovely that she made even pretty women, such as her two older sisters, seem homely. She seemed like a perfect marble statue come to life.

[1] (sī′ kē)

Psyche's parents, a king and queen, were very proud of their daughter. They greedily schemed to have her marry the richest king in the land.

Every day, men would **throng** the hallways of the palace just to catch a glimpse of lovely Psyche. They'd present her with flowers, jewelry, or rare perfumes. They gladly offered anything for just one smile from this beauty. For them, she was an earthly Venus.[2] In fact, they even dared to call her by the name of the goddess of love and beauty.

Naturally the real Venus soon discovered something was wrong. She first began to suspect trouble when she visited her altars and temples. There she found cold ashes heaped where warm fires used to crackle. Tall weeds grew in place of flowers. And the fountains were turning gray and dirty because no one scrubbed the stone surfaces.

The goddess finally found out why she was being neglected. All the mortals were paying **homage** to Psyche instead!

Immediately Venus was filled with jealousy and hatred for the mortal girl. She quickly formed a plot and sought out her son Cupid[3] for help. She found the handsome boy polishing his love-poisoned arrows.

"My son, I need your help at once. My temples are in a shambles. Humans have stopped making sacrifices to me. And all because of a stupid mortal named Psyche!"

Venus stomped her lovely feet. "How dare she pretend to match my beauty? How dare she accept the gifts and honors that are rightly mine? This cannot continue! I want you to use your power and make the wretch fall in love with the ugliest creature alive. Go now. You will find her asleep in the palace below."

Cupid gave his mother a puzzled stare. "Mother, the girl can only fall in love with the one she sees when the arrow strikes her. How will you arrange for your creature to be nearby when she awakens?"

[2](vē′ nus)
[3](kū′ pid)

Venus impatiently waved her hand. "Leave that to me. I'll be sure that the first creature she sets eyes upon will be quite special." Venus gave a sly smile.

Cupid shrugged his shoulders. "Well, it seems pretty cruel to me, Mother. But I'll do as you wish."

Cupid put the shiny arrows into his quiver[4] and slung it over his shoulder. Then he unfolded his gorgeous wings and took flight.

Cupid easily found the palace and landed at Psyche's window. After making himself invisible, he slipped into her room.

Inside he found Psyche asleep. The moon **illuminated** her lovely face.

Cupid stopped and stared. He couldn't move. Never in all his long life had he seen a lovelier creature. For you see, like many sons, he never really thought of his mother's beauty.

Many times before, Cupid had let his arrows fly into human hearts. It was his job. But now, his arms raised, the arrow positioned, he couldn't do it. Not to this creature. He didn't want this lovely girl to fall victim to his mother's evil plan.

Cupid lowered his bow and stared some more. So intent was he that he didn't notice the arrow slipping off the bow. Before he realized it, the arrow was free. Straight into his foot it plunged!

At once Cupid felt the sweet poison spread through his veins. He felt his heart swell with passion. Then he grew numb and dizzy with great joy. So this must be what love felt like!

Psyche stirred. She was beginning to awaken. Cupid didn't dare stay a minute longer. Though it broke his newly awakened heart, he turned and flew back to Mt. Olympus.[5]

---

[4] A quiver is a round, narrow holder for arrows.

[5] (ō lim′ pus) Mt. Olympus is where most of the major Greek gods were said to live.

For days Cupid thought and dreamed only of Psyche. All too soon those lovely dreams were interrupted by Venus. The goddess had been expecting Psyche to fall in love with the ugly wretch she had sent. Finally, weary of waiting, Venus sought out her son.

"Why didn't Psyche fall in love with my monster? Didn't you do as I ordered?"

"No," Cupid calmly answered.

Venus' voice grew harsher as she tried to contain her anger. "And why not?"

"Because I have fallen in love with her. And I couldn't let such an ugly fate happen to such a lovely maiden."

Venus no longer tried to control herself. "Out of my sight! The god of love struck by one of his own arrows? Let's hope the other gods haven't heard your news. Why, you'd be the laughingstock of Mt. Olympus! And then they would laugh at me!"

In vain Cupid tried to interrupt. But Venus angrily shook her head. "No! No explanations! Just go! And don't come near me again until this silliness has left you!"

Being ordered to leave made no difference to Cupid. He could dream about his love anywhere. So he took flight without another word.

But Venus was far from satisfied. She would teach her foolish son and that rude girl. She would teach them to respect her. Let them both find out what it meant to be in **disfavor**!

So Venus set about putting her second plan into effect. And soon a strange thing began to happen in Psyche's kingdom. Every young woman but herself was getting married. Many men still filed past Psyche's palace, but none asked for her hand. Even Psyche's older sisters were married off to rich kings. But there sat Psyche, the most beautiful girl in the land, quite alone.

When Cupid saw how lonely Psyche seemed, he darted back to Mt. Olympus.

"How dare you make Psyche an outcast in her own land!" he shouted at his mother when he found her. "You've put a spell on her so that no man asks for her hand! So she sits unwanted and unloved!"

Venus smiled. "Would you rather have her being offered and *accepting* a marriage offer?"

This enraged Cupid. "Jealous, that's what you are! All humans should worship Psyche's beauty! But you can't stop me from adoring her. And until you accept that fact, you'll have seen the last of me."

Concern began to dawn on Venus' face. "Oh, yes," Cupid added gleefully. "You're beginning to see, aren't you, Mother? Think of it. No one will fall in love! And no one will sing your praises. You'll soon find out what it's like to be in Psyche's place!"

Cupid didn't let his mother reply. He leaped into the air and was gone.

Cupid made good on his promise to Venus. All creatures stopped falling in love. No marriages were celebrated and no babies were born. No flowers bloomed, no plants budded, and no animals mated. Farmers, hunters, servants—everyone—did their jobs with a heavy heart. The world had become a desert of emotion. And once again, Venus' temples and altars were neglected.

Venus saw all this and realized she was beaten. She sent a message to Cupid. In a very short time, the determined god was back.

"Very well, son. You win," Venus coldly announced. "I hate being ignored! I'll give you anything you want."

"I want Psyche," Cupid simply replied.

"As you wish. May the girl be worth your efforts," said Venus. "Now hurry back to your work and return love to the world."

Cupid smiled and repeated his mother's words. "As you wish."

Cupid once again showered the world with arrows. As when water floods a dry river during a summer rain, so life gushed back into the world.

But love did not return to all. Venus had still not lifted her spell on Psyche. So the maiden remained alone and unmarried.

Naturally this began to concern Psyche's parents. Her father finally traveled to the oracle of Apollo.[6] He hoped he would find advice there about finding a good husband for Psyche.

But the king received some shocking news. The oracle told him, "No mortal man is going to marry your daughter. She is destined for a being greater than man. Take her to the mountaintop and bid her farewell."

The king wept all the way home. He was certain his daughter was meant as a sacrifice to some monster. Yet though he grieved, he dared not protest the oracle.

At home, the king could scarcely bear to report the oracle's words. However, Psyche did not even shed a tear when she heard the news. Instead, she stood up and bravely said, "There is nothing for me here but heartache. I may as well meet my fate elsewhere. Let us leave tonight."

That night the wind picked up. It blew in great gusts, hurling bushes and tearing branches. But Psyche was determined to go, no matter what the weather.

So Psyche and her family and some people of the kingdom set off for the mountain. Many muttered and shook beneath the blasts of wind. A few even fell back and returned to their homes. But Psyche went forward without a word.

When they reached the top of the mountain, Psyche finally turned and spoke. Looking at the **somber** faces around her, she said, "For years you have delighted in my beauty. But I can say now that it has given me little pleasure. I have felt like a hollow shell—a statue of Venus, as you have dared to call me. And that has been my downfall, I fear. Go now. I want to meet my fate alone."

[6](a pol' lō) Apollo was the god of truth, archery, medicine, and music. People came to his oracle at Delphi to hear the truth or the future revealed.

Psyche watched until the group was out of sight. Then she climbed to the uppermost peak. Wrapping her robe round her, she sat down and faced the great **abyss** below.

Despite the howling wind and sharp rocks, Psyche was calm. This was the first time in her life she felt totally free. Free from smothering crowds. Free from **adulation**. Free from her beauty. Out in the wild, it didn't matter whether one was beautiful or plain. That was nice for a change.

But soon other thoughts began to run through Psyche's mind. What exactly did the oracle mean by the words "destined for a being greater than man"? What was her husband going to be? A monster? A giant?

Or was the husband part just a trick to get her to this mountain? Maybe she was actually meant to be a sacrifice to the gods.

Psyche shivered. In part, the chill wind caused her to shake. But she also was bothered by her thoughts.

Suddenly the temperature changed. The wind shifted and turned warm and gentle.

Psyche realized that Zephyr[7] must be near. He was the sweetest and kindest of all the winds.

Closer and closer the god came. And with each step, the wind grew stronger. Psyche's robes began stirring again.

All at once, Psyche felt herself lifted into the air. Zephyr was completely supporting her weight!

Breathless with shock, Psyche watched as she floated down the mountain. On and on the wind carried her. She flew over valleys, forests, and then more mountains.

As she drifted over the miles of landscape, Psyche began to enjoy the ride. What a beautiful view she had!

At last Zephyr set her gently down in a grassy meadow and departed. Psyche gazed around her in wonder. But at that moment, the moon darted beneath a cloud. So among some sweet-smelling flowers, Psyche settled down for the night. Before long, she had drifted into sleep.

Psyche awoke the next morning to see millions of blue

[7](zef′ ir)

and white flowers. They dotted the landscape as far as she could see.

As she turned to view more of her new world, Psyche caught her breath. Next to a rushing river stood a glorious palace.

Hope stirred again in Psyche's breast. Might her husband-to-be live there? Surely only a being greater than man could own such a palace! Excited and curious, Psyche headed for the entrance.

When she arrived, the huge gates swung open without a noise. Psyche entered and stared. Not a soul could be seen. Yet everything was gorgeous and sparkling. The palace looked as though hundreds of servants had just polished it all.

And how rich everything was! Golden pillars held up golden ceilings. And between the silver walls stretched a floor **embedded** with priceless gems. She was standing on diamonds, pearls, and emeralds larger than her hand!

A voice from nowhere softly spoke to her. "This is your new home, my lady. We, your servants, welcome you. Ask anything and we shall bring it or perform it. Whatever you wish is yours for the asking.

"Now if you would like to visit your room, a bath awaits you. And your breakfast is ready whenever you choose."

The same soft voice led Psyche to her room. There she was once again struck by the mix of comfort, riches, and beauty. Gratefully she sank into the warm water of her huge bath.

After she finished bathing and dressing, Psyche found she was hungry. Quietly she called, "If you please, I would like to eat now."

Immediately a set table appeared. Then just as mysteriously, food drifted to her plate. At the same time, wine filled the goblet. Psyche sat down and ate the delicious meal. Invisible musicians kept her company with lovely songs.

After eating, Psyche strolled out into the gardens around the palace. With childlike joy, she explored the paths and gathered flowers.

Psyche enjoyed herself very much that day. Yet she was also bothered by a strange feeling. The feeling eventually grew into a **conviction** that she was being followed. Several times she turned around. Yet no one was ever behind her. At least no one visible.

Was it just the servants? Psyche didn't think so. Somehow, she felt that the hidden being was the one the oracle had spoken of.

That night, Psyche ate in the garden. Then as the moon rose, she went to her room. She stretched out on her comfortable bed and blew out the last candle.

Presently a soft voice came out of the dark. It was a male voice, friendly and soothing.

"Welcome to my palace, dearest Psyche. At long last, welcome," Cupid said. For, of course, it was the young god.

He spoke gently. Yet Psyche felt as though lightning had struck her heart.

"Oh, who are you, kind lord? Please, who are you?" she whispered.

"Lovely Psyche, I am your husband. I have waited so long to be in your arms."

"And now hearing your voice, it seems as though I've been waiting my whole life for you," replied Psyche. "How can this be, my lord? Surely the gods must have brought us together. For already I love you with all my heart. Where are you, my husband?"

"Here, dear wife." Psyche felt Cupid's muscular body slip into her outstretched arms. She sighed with deep contentment. He smelled so sweet, like a meadow at dawn. And his skin was smoother than the richest fabric.

Cupid whispered, "You have been very brave, my love. Making your night journey to the mountain. Sending the others away. Then letting Zephyr bring you here. Your soul is as beautiful as your face. I shall love you forever, dear wife."

Psyche had been praised by thousands of men in thousands of ways. But she had never heard such sweet words. "This must be love," she thought to herself. She tightened her arms round her husband.

When Psyche awoke the next morning, she was alone. But she didn't care. She knew her husband would be back.

All day long she danced in the gardens. Over and over she recalled her husband's tender words.

By nightfall, she could think of nothing but her husband. So she was delighted that the moment the candle was out, Cupid was beside her. In his arms, she felt so happy. She wondered which god to thank for such a husband.

Days and nights passed like this. Sometimes Psyche feared that her lovely life might be only a dream. But soon she was calmed by her love for Cupid.

Psyche felt her life was almost perfect. Just one thing bothered her. So one night she **broached** her concern.

"Dear husband, I only see you at night," she said. "And then I don't see you at all really. Is there some reason you wish to remain hidden?"

"Aren't the emotions you feel better than what you might see, dear wife?" came his reply. "Believe me, your heart is much more reliable than your eyes. And twice as honest. Weren't there times when you wished you could cover yourself? Just to see if people loved you for yourself, not your beauty?"

Psyche was not surprised Cupid knew her deepest wishes. It seemed they spoke, acted, and even dreamed as one.

Cupid continued, "Would you want me to adore you only for your beauty? Because I confess, dear Psyche, I first was attracted by your loveliness. But now after knowing you, I realize how much more I love you for your spirit."

"I would rather have your respect than ten thousand compliments about my face," Psyche admitted.

"Well, you understand then. I also do not wish to be judged by my appearance. No, judge me by my actions and your own heart."

Psyche knew this was very important to him. "Agreed, dear husband. It does not matter what you look like. As for your actions, you have treated me like a goddess. And my heart . . . . Well, it is the happiest in all the land."

They lovingly curled into each other's arms and slept.

Yet with that cloud past, a new worry came to Psyche. More and more she thought about her family. She wondered if they were happy. Had they stopped **mourning** for her? She longed to see her sisters again. She wanted them to know she was happy and in love.

Finally Psyche's longing overwhelmed her. So she asked Cupid if her sisters could visit.

Cupid hesitated for a moment. At once Psyche suspected he was holding something back. Yet when he spoke, he granted her wish. "For you, my wife, I would do anything," he vowed.

Cupid kept his promise. The very next day, Zephyr brought Psyche's sisters to her doorstep. The women were terrified at being snatched from their own palaces. They were even more amazed to see Psyche, whom they believed dead.

Psyche was so happy to see her sisters, tears ran down her face. She hugged them for a long time before realizing she hadn't even invited them inside.

Psyche was quite proud of her home. She danced from room to room, showing her sisters one precious item after another. The sisters stared in wonder. Time and again they reached out to touch a treasure. And each time they felt certain it would pop like a soap bubble.

Eventually Psyche led her sisters into the garden. "Are you hungry, dear sisters? For I have a feast in store for you."

The two older women glanced at each other. "We were wondering where your servants were. We didn't see any the entire time we were inside. We hoped that you had some help."

"Oh, I have help," Psyche said with a smile. "Let me show you."

Her sisters stared at Psyche as she spoke to the air. "We shall dine in the garden today."

At once a table and chairs for three appeared. Goblets and plates appeared as well.

Psyche's sisters stared with open mouths. She had to lead them by the hands to get them to the table.

Psyche laughed. "My servants are perhaps the greatest treasure in the palace. They are always at hand and yet never underfoot. They also are very talented musicians. Would you like music with your meal?"

With **bemused** looks, the sisters nodded.

Psyche spoke into the air again. "Could we have music, please?"

A lyre[8] began playing. And as the music drifted through the garden, the sisters recovered from their shock. Slowly at first and then more quickly, they ate the heavenly food.

Yet once in a while, Psyche's sisters had trouble swallowing. For in place of their wonder, bitter jealousy was growing. In fact, they had always been jealous of their younger sister. Her beauty had outshone theirs from the moment of her birth.

Now here was Psyche, enjoying treasures the gods would envy! Their husbands, who were both rich kings, couldn't afford even one room of Psyche's palace.

At the thought of husbands, a little gleam came into the eye of the eldest. She traded a quick glance with the second eldest. Then she spoke.

"Psyche, we have been so greedy! Why, we completely forgot to wait dinner for your husband!"

Psyche went pale and lowered her goblet. "I—I—My husband is away hunting."

"Oh?" replied the eldest doubtfully. "So he likes to hunt? You know, that's the first thing you've mentioned about him." At that, Psyche grew even paler.

The second sister leaned across the table. With a voice full of false concern, she asked, "Dear sister, is something wrong? Perhaps you're not as close as you should be? Perhaps you don't love him?"

---

[8]A lyre is a harplike instrument.

"With all my heart I love him," answered Psyche.

"Well, every new bride I've known couldn't stop talking about her husband," said the middle sister. "And that's especially true if he's as wealthy as yours seems to be."

"Yes," agreed the older sister. "And every new bride I've known has loved to praise her husband's looks. What does your husband look like, Psyche?"

"He is the most beautiful—" stammered Psyche. "He is the most beautiful being I've ever known. You should be happy for me, sisters."

"A 'being'? What do you mean by that? He is a man, isn't he?"

The eldest turned to the middle sister. "Maybe what the oracle said is true. Her husband is some kind of beast." They spoke as if Psyche were not even present.

Then they turned back to Psyche. With one question after another they **assaulted** Psyche.

Finally she broke down. "Please, please, stop!" she cried. "I'll tell you the truth. I've never seen him! He comes to me only at night. He could be anything—I don't know! But I do know he's beautiful. Beautiful beyond words."

"Beautiful things like to be seen, Psyche. Just look at you."

"Yes, you used to sit in the window just waiting for the crowds to appear," the other sister chimed in. "You loved to be on display!"

Psyche was so shocked, she didn't know what to say. She'd hated being pointed at and treated like an object!

Before she could reply, the same sister continued. "Only a creature who has something to hide would refuse to be seen by day. I'm afraid you've married a monster, dear sister."

"How dare you speak of my husband in such a way!" cried Psyche. "You know nothing about him! Nothing except what your jealous minds have imagined!"

The elder sister shook her head, as though in great sadness. "Jealous? No, little sister. Just concerned." She sighed and leaned back. "Of course, you're entitled to your secrets. You don't have to prove anything to us, Psyche."

"Of course not," the second sister chimed in. "But what about yourself? I think you're the one with doubts, sister. So why not light a candle tonight? Just to see what your love looks like. What could be the harm in that?"

Psyche stood up, shaking with anger. "Keep your hateful suggestions to yourself! I'm sorry that I invited you here! I am even sorrier that I wept and rejoiced at your coming. Now I only want you to go and never come back!"

Zephyr was close by and heard Psyche's wish. Before the sisters could even rise from the table, he had whisked them away. This time he gave them a wild, bumpy ride before dumping them at their palaces.

The rest of that day, Psyche stayed in her room. She didn't feel like walking through her gardens. She didn't even request her evening meal. She simply paced back and forth, **brooding** about her sisters' words:

" 'I think you're the one with doubts, sister. So why not light a candle tonight? Just to see what your love looks like. What could be the harm in that?' "

As much as Psyche hated to admit it, her sisters did have a point. What could be the harm in one look? That's all she'd need. Just one look at her beloved husband's face.

"No, I mustn't," Psyche argued aloud. "He trusts me. It's the only thing he's asked of me."

But as the hours wore on, she grew more convinced by her sisters' arguments. If her husband weren't a monster, why wouldn't he show himself? She had begged him. Yet he still wouldn't let himself be seen. If he truly loved her, he would show himself just to satisfy her curiosity.

He must be a monster! Psyche trembled at the thought. She had shared her bed with who knows what kind of creature!

With that terrible thought, Psyche decided. She would see her husband's face tonight!

At dusk, Psyche slipped into bed. As always, she blew

out the candle. Then she lay with her eyes open, waiting for nightfall.

When the last spark of light faded, Psyche felt her husband slip into bed beside her. If Cupid had even kissed her, Psyche would have given up her plan. But her thoughtful husband, who didn't want to wake her, never even brushed her lips. So Psyche's fear remained greater than her love.

Psyche listened as Cupid's breath became even and slow. Then she crawled out of bed and lit the candle. The poor girl also grabbed a knife. If some fearsome monster awaited her, she would be prepared.

As the flame **wavered** in her shaking hand, Psyche tiptoed back to the bed. She shone the light on her husband's face and gave a gasp.

There was a god sleeping in her bed! And a bow and quiver rested on the floor!

Cupid was her husband? Cupid, the god of love?

Psyche breathed a sigh of relief. Then she leaned closer for another look. His beauty took her breath away. His face was so youthful, so strong, so handsome! Shining golden hair ringed his face. And a pair of pure white wings were folded behind his shoulders.

But Psyche had leaned too close. Before she could catch it, the candle tipped in her hand. A large drop of hot wax fell onto Cupid's shoulder.

Cupid awoke with a start and looked straight into Psyche's eyes. It was as if he were reading her mind. Then in a flash, he had seized the candle and blown it out. Next moment he was out of bed and on his feet.

Psyche reached out to hold him. But he pushed her away and lifted into the air.

"No! Please, dear husband! Don't leave me!" Psyche cried.

Cupid's voice came from the window ledge. "Did I have to be beautiful for you to love me, dear wife?"

"No!" Psyche shouted. "I loved you before!"

"No, Psyche. If you had truly loved me, you wouldn't have had to see my face. You would have trusted your heart."

With that, Cupid flew out the window into the night air. Psyche ran into the courtyard after him. She tried to follow the sound of his voice.

"True beauty lies in the heart. That is why I loved you, Psyche. Your heart was beautiful. But it has grown ugly from fear and doubt. And love cannot live where the heart does not trust. Farewell."

A big whoosh of wind made Psyche turn around. The palace had disappeared! The gardens were gone! All the remains of her delightful life vanished with Love.[9]

Psyche ran to the grassy meadow where Zephyr had first set her down. She called out to him and then leaped into the air. But this time the god did not come to carry her. Psyche fell to the ground and wept.

When she had exhausted her tears, Psyche's strong spirit reawakened. At once she set off on a search for Cupid. Many dangers she faced along the way. But Psyche didn't fear death. The pain in her heart told her there were far worse things.

Psyche's search continued for days and then weeks. Finally she realized it was hopeless to search for her husband on earth. She would have to go to Olympus itself. Better yet, she should seek out Venus.

At once Psyche went to one of Venus' temples. She didn't even have to call out, for the angry goddess was waiting.

"So you dare to come crawling here!" Venus scolded. "After you tried to take my place as goddess of beauty! After you betrayed and wounded—yes, actually wounded—my son!"

Psyche stared back, pale and numb.

"What he sees in you, I can't understand. Such an ugly girl. Really, the comparisons between us are laughable. The only possible value you have as a wife would be in

[9]Cupid was also known as Love.

housekeeping. If you were good at such things . . . . Well, perhaps you might convince me that you were worth something to Cupid, after all. As a servant perhaps. Shall we put you to the test?'' Venus asked.

But it wasn't a question. Psyche knew she dare not refuse. Not if she hoped ever to see Cupid again.

The great goddess led her to the storehouse of her temple. With an **imperious** gesture, she said, ''Sort these seeds into separate piles, girl. And do it by nightfall.''

Psyche stared in despair at the heap of seeds. Thousands upon thousands of seeds were mixed together. She could never do it by nightfall.

Yet do it she tried. And as she sifted the seeds, she noticed black spots swarming before her eyes.

Was she losing her sight? She rubbed her tired head and looked again. No, the spots were ants. As the astonished Psyche watched, the little creatures moved over the pile of seeds. With quick **efficiency**, they sorted the grain. By the time Venus came back, the one huge pile had been turned into twenty smaller ones.

Venus frowned when she saw the neatly sorted piles. ''Well, you've managed somehow, little fool. But I don't think you did it by yourself. Tomorrow we'll see if you're so lucky.'' Throwing a crust of bread to the girl, she marched out.

In the morning, Venus was ready with another grim task. ''At the riverbank are a herd of sheep with golden wool. Bring me back a basket full of their wool at once.''

Psyche went to the river, once again determined to try. But again, someone was watching over her, for the river god spoke up. ''Psyche, don't go near the sheep whose wool you seek. Those fierce creatures will tear you to pieces.''

''But how am I to get their wool?'' she asked.

''Among the bushes nearby, you'll find what you seek. The thorns catch the wool when the sheep **browse** there.''

Psyche did as the river god suggested and gathered a heaping bushel of wool. But, of course, the present didn't please Venus.

"So you have completed another of my tasks," said Venus. "Or have *you*? Well, perhaps you can try this next task by yourself. Go to the waterfall beyond those dark hills. Fill this pitcher with water and return to me."

When Psyche reached the falls, she paused in bewilderment. How could she ever get down these steep, jagged rocks to the falls? And once down there, how could she get back up?

"Try," she told herself. "You must try for his sake."

Biting her lips, Psyche moved forward. But just as she was about to start down, an eagle flew up. Snatching the pitcher from her hand, it darted toward the waterfall. Then dipping into the falls, it filled the jug. Before Psyche could even whisper a prayer, the eagle was back.

When Psyche returned from this mission, Venus glared at the girl. "Another job done. And I suppose you're expecting to rest? Ah, if only I could. Day and night I've been nursing dear Cupid. I don't know when he'll ever recover from that nasty burn you gave him."

Psyche knew Venus was lying just to torment her. Yet she couldn't keep her worry and shame from showing.

Venus laughed. "Such a face, silly child. It reminds me that my own beauty isn't quite what it should be. All those long hours at my son's side."

The goddess clapped her hands, as though suddenly thinking of an idea. "What I need is some help from Proserpina.[10] With her looks, she can surely spare me some of her beauty. Anyway, she's buried in the Underworld with that gloomy husband of hers. What does she need it all for?"

Venus grabbed a box and shoved it into Psyche's hands. "Hurry now and fetch some for me."

Psyche was utterly lost. How did you get to Hades? And

[10] (pro ser' pi na) The goddess Proserpina was married to Hades (hā' dēz), god of the Underworld (also called Hades).

once there, how did you get through and back?

Psyche decided to look for the entrance to the Underworld from a high tower nearby. Again, some kindly god stepped in to help. This time the spirit of the tower told her how to safely reach Proserpina.

Psyche listened carefully and did all that her mysterious guide suggested. Through a hole in the earth she went. Then she crossed a dark river in Charon's[11] ferry. She also passed a fierce, three-headed dog after first throwing him a cake.[12]

Finally she found Proserpina. That goddess, lovely as autumn flowers, placed some of her beauty in the box. With many thanks, Psyche quickly left and returned to her own daylight world.

Yet even as she prepared to enter Venus' temple, Psyche paused. Longingly she looked at the box in her hand.

"Oh, how I wish I had some of Proserpina's beauty," she murmured. "How ugly I must seem with my cut hands and feet, dirty face, and red eyes. Will Cupid ever bother to look at me again? Surely a little of this beauty wouldn't be missed. I wonder what it looks like?"

Psyche cracked open the box. With a nervous glance, she peered inside. It was empty!

The thought barely occurred to Psyche before she fell to her knees. Exhaustion poured over her. Almost instantly she fell into a **stupor**. While Proserpina's beauty might suit a goddess, it cast mortals into a deep sleep.

But once again, rescue was near. All along Cupid had been keeping a watchful eye on his wife. In fact, he was the one who saw that others helped Psyche through each task.

When Cupid saw Psyche fall to the ground, he was out the window at once. Forgotten were his pride and anger. All he could remember were Psyche's loving eyes.

In a moment, he was by Psyche's side. A gentle touch from one of his arrows broke the spell. Slowly Psyche stirred

---

[11] (ka' ron) With his ferryboat, Charon carried the souls of the dead into Hades.
[12] The three-headed dog Cerberus guarded the gates of the Underworld.

and opened her eyes. Then as she stared up at him in wonder, he gathered her into his arms.

"My husband!" she cried in delight.

"Dear, dear Psyche," he murmured. "So brave, so lovely, so loyal. And so curious. How I love you."

After a long kiss, Cupid released her. "Now go to my mother and complete your task. I will be busy with my own mission."

Cupid flew at once to Olympus and sought out Jupiter.[13] If anyone could end these games of his mother's, it would be the king of the gods.

Briefly Cupid explained what had happened. Then he made his request.

Jupiter smiled at the young god. "It's pleasant to see you in the role of the lover. I hope your suffering makes you go easier on the rest of us next time you shoot an arrow."

Cupid started to protest anxiously. But Jupiter waved his hand. "Yes, yes, boy. It's your job. And mine is to pass judgment. Today, the scales tip in your favor. Your request is granted. Fetch your wife here."

With a joyful exclamation, Cupid flew off. In no time he had returned with Psyche.

After the young wife was bathed and freshly dressed, she was **ushered** to Jupiter's throne. With the eye of a true lover of beauty, Jupiter looked her up and down.

Finally he said, "Your husband has told me of your bravery. You have the form to match your soul, my dear. Such beauty must not be allowed to fade." He gestured and a god brought forward a cup of nectar.

"Drink that, Psyche. Drink it and become immortal, like your husband. For there is an invisible cord which ties your hearts together. May it remain unbroken to the end of time!"

With those words, the wedding feasting began. All the gods came—even Venus. Selfish and jealous as she was, the goddess knew when to give in. After all, no one can defeat the most powerful force in the universe: Love.

[13] (jū' pi ter)

INSIGHTS

Does this myth seem familiar? Perhaps you've read other versions of this story such as "Beauty and the Beast." It's fitting that Psyche's story has been adapted to fairy tales, for it has many fairy tale elements. Evil older sisters, magic, separated lovers, quests, and animal helpers are a few of those features. Another element is not all that common in Greek mythology: a happy ending.

Psyche has a fitting and lovely name. In Greek, it means *soul*. Words such as *psychology* and *psychic* come from the same root, though they relate more to the mind than the soul.

Psyche also means *butterfly* in Greek. Artists often picture Psyche with butterfly wings. This is not only a play on her name but symbolizes the change she undergoes.

Zephyr is the name of the gentle west wind that rescues Psyche. Today the word refers to any warm, mild breeze. It also served as a poetic name for a train.

Many artists picture Cupid as a plump child. And in some myths, Cupid did remain a child for a long time.

This fact didn't please Venus. She finally learned from Themis, a seer, that Cupid would only grow if he had a brother. In due time, Venus' next son, Anteros, was born. And as predicted, Cupid grew stronger and taller.

As for Anteros, he carried on in the family tradition. He became the avenger of unhappy love.

Morals certainly change over the centuries. As the symbol of earthly as well as holy love, Venus was the goddess of prostitutes.

This side of Venus' nature is best seen at Cornith. Her temple there was filled with prostitutes. These women gave their fees to the priests. And since the women's prayers were felt to be very powerful, they also prayed for those who needed help.

Since the prostitutes brought Cornith a lot of money, they were greatly valued. In fact, grateful worshippers often gave prostitutes to the temple instead of money.

JASON AND THE GOLDEN FLEECE

VOCABULARY PREVIEW

Below is a list of words that appear in the story. Read the list and get to know the words before you start the story.

craved—desired; longed for
exile—removal from one's homeland
fated—decided beforehand; destined
fleece—the wool covering of a sheep
formidable—fearsome; dreadful
incantations—magic words or chants
invincible—unable to be overcome; unconquerable
peril—great risk or danger
predicament—a difficult or troubling situation
prophecies—statements that tell the future
quest—a journey to search for something
rapt—paying complete attention; absorbed
refrain—withhold; stop
rekindled—lighted again
sorceress—witch; female magician
threshold—doorway; entrance
traitorous—unfaithful; betraying
trifle—thing of little value or importance
vanity—too much pride in oneself
vitality—energy

JASON
and the
GOLDEN
FLEECE

Magical armies of soldiers,
a watchful dragon,
murderous relatives,
and an angry giant.
Those are some of the challenges
awaiting Jason on his quest for the
Golden Fleece.
Yet the greatest danger
is one Jason never sees
until far too
late.

Heroes seek adventure for countless reasons. Sometimes it's for honor only—the honor of homeland, ruler, or gods. Other times it's in defense of home and family. The hope of glory, wealth, and fame spurs others on. Heroes seldom do heroic things without a reason.

But what about a man who desires mainly the adventure itself? What reward does he bring home from his travels?

Jason was such a man, one who lived mostly for the thrill of danger. This is the story of his **quest** for the Golden Fleece and what came from that quest.

Jason's adventures began when his father, Aeson, grew weary of ruling his kingdom, Thessaly.[1] So he decided to retire. Most unwisely, he gave up his kingdom to his wicked nephew, Pelias.[2]

At that time, Jason was growing up in a faraway land. When he heard the news about Pelias, he came to a decision. Jason knew that he, not Pelias, should rule in his father's place. So when he reached adulthood, he went home to claim the throne.

Pelias was not pleased by Jason's visit. He was reminded of two **prophecies**. The first said that he would be killed by a relative. The other told him to beware of a man wearing one sandal. Whether on purpose or by accident, Jason came with one foot bare.

Staring at that bare foot, Pelias coldly asked Jason, "Who are you? Why have you come?"

"I am your cousin, Aeson's son," Jason replied. "I've come to claim what's rightfully mine. Let's not fight over this kingdom. That isn't worthy of noble Greeks. I'll let you keep all the lands and wealth you've taken. Just give me my father's throne."

"Very well," said Pelias slyly. "But kindly do me one favor first. The people of Colchis[3] possess a wonderful treasure, the Golden **Fleece**. It belonged to our poor lost cousin Phrixus.[4] So by rights, it's truly ours. Go fetch it for me. Then you shall have your kingdom."

Jason didn't have to think it over. He heartily agreed. He recalled the story of the magnificent Golden Fleece. It

[1] (ē′ son) (thes′ sa lē)
[2] (pē′ li as)
[3] (kol′ kis)
[4] (frik′ sus)

came from a magical ram who saved Phrixus from being sacrificed by his wicked stepmother. The ram carried Phrixus safely to King Aeetes'[5] land of Colchis. There the grateful Phrixus sacrificed the ram to the gods. Then he gave its fleece to Aeetes. The king hung the Golden Fleece from a tree guarded by a dragon that never slept.

But the Golden Fleece wasn't really what fascinated Jason. His heart soared with the thought of adventure. After all, he knew the world only from his books of childhood. This was a chance to see wonderful things and places for himself.

The Golden Fleece didn't matter much to Pelias, either. He knew the treasure wasn't rightfully his and didn't expect to obtain it. What he really wished for was Jason's death. He knew the quest would be filled with **peril**. He thought, "Surely, this fellow will never return alive."

.However, Jason was determined to do just that. He asked Argus,[6] a famous carpenter, to build a fifty-oared ship. Though quite a workman, Argus could hardly believe his ears. The Greeks of that time traveled only in small boats.

Still, like Jason, Argus loved a challenge. So he set about his work. Soon the ship—named the *Argo*[7] after its maker—was finished.

Next, Jason called for volunteers to serve as his crew. Hundreds of fine men answered. Jason was able to choose many of the bravest and strongest. Among these was Heracles,[8] the strongest man on earth. Orpheus,[9] the great poet and musician, was another. Castor and Pollux,[10] the daring twins, also signed aboard. Well-satisfied, Jason set sail with his courageous crew of Argonauts.[11]

[5] (ē ē′ tēz)

[6] (ar′ gus)

[7] (ar′ gō)

[8] (her′ a klēz)

[9] (or′ fūs or or′ fē us)

[10] (kas′ tor) (pol′ lux)

[11] (ar′ gō notz) *Argonauts* combines the name of Jason's ship and the Greek word *naut* which means "sailor."

The gods often played unseen parts in stories of great heroes. So it was in the story of Jason and the Argonauts. Hera, Zeus' wife and queen of the gods, was fond of Jason.[12] She saw to it that he had fair winds and good fortune. Hera was willful and short-tempered, so it was better to have her on your side than against you.

The Argonauts landed first on the island of Lemnos,[13] where only women lived. The women had killed all their men. They spared only their elderly king. Him they put into a hollow chest, which they pushed out to sea. Although they didn't know it, the lucky king reached safety in a distant land.

The Argonauts were uneasy to find themselves among such **formidable** hostesses. Yet they were treated well. The women supplied them with food and clothing for the long voyage ahead.

All went well—until Heracles ran into trouble. Heracles was a prize member of Jason's crew. He was a courageous and loyal fellow. Apart from adventure, he was most devoted to friends.

Heracles had a cabin boy named Hylas,[14] who went ashore one day for water. Hylas soon found a spring and dipped his pitcher into it. As he did so, a nymph[15] under the water saw how handsome the boy was. She quickly reached up and pulled Hylas into the spring. He was never seen again.

When Hylas did not return, Heracles went ashore in search of him. "Hylas, where are you!" he bellowed, plunging into the woods. "Come out at once, or you'll get the beating of your life!"

Despite this show of anger, Heracles wept inwardly for his lost friend. He was so grief-stricken, in fact, that he forgot about his companions. He vanished into the woods. The Argonauts were finally forced to leave without him.

---

[12] (hē′ ra or her′ a) (zūs)
[13] (lem′ nos)
[14] (hī′ las)
[15] (nimf) Nymphs were lesser goddesses who lived in forests and streams.

At their next landing, they met an unfortunate old prophet named Phineus.[16] Zeus, the king of gods, wasn't fond of this prophet. Phineus had revealed a secret that Zeus wanted to keep.

So Zeus had come up with a cruel punishment for Phineus by setting the Harpies[17] upon him. These "hounds of Zeus" were vulture-like creatures with terrible claws. They left a sickening smell wherever they went. To torture Phineus, the Harpies would appear whenever he was about to eat. Then they would wolf down almost all his food. The few morsels which remained were too foul to eat.

Jason's men found the old man wasting away from starvation. But, being a prophet, Phineus knew that two of the Argonauts were **fated** to save him. His rescuers were to be the sons of Boreas,[18] the great North Wind.

So when Phineus' next meal was set, the brave brothers stood beside him with drawn swords. The Harpies appeared almost at once. After making quick work of Phineus' table, they flew away. But in hot pursuit behind them were the sons of Boreas. They hacked away at the creatures and were about to kill them. But suddenly Iris, the goddess of the rainbow, appeared and stepped between them.

"Why do you stop us?" complained the brothers. "We're fated to save Phineus. Leave us to do our work."

"You've done your work already," said the goddess. "Now kindly **refrain** from killing Zeus' precious hounds. Phineus shall never be disturbed by them again. You have my promise!"

The sons of Boreas believed the goddess' words. They returned to Phineus to tell him the good news. To celebrate, the prophet and the Argonauts feasted all night.

The next morning, the grateful Phineus asked, "How can I repay you?"

[16](fin′ ē us or fī′ nūs)
[17](har′ pēz)
[18](bō′ rē as)

Wisely, the Argonauts asked him what dangers lay ahead.

"Beware of the Symplegades[19]—the Clashing Islands," Phineus told them. "These rocks float upon the sea, tossing and crashing together. They destroy anything which comes between them. When you reach them, send a dove ahead of you. If the bird returns from the Symplegades, the way is safe."

The Argonauts set sail the next morning. And sure enough, they soon came to the Symplegades. The islands were even more threatening than they had imagined. They stirred up the sea with their clashing. Anything that came between them was crushed.

The Argonauts freed a dove and watched her fly toward the Clashing Islands. She quickly vanished from sight. But just as quickly, she returned—and with only a few tail feathers lost. The Argonauts then knew the way would be safe.

Still, it was a terrifying passage. They were almost past danger when the islands began to close upon them. The Argonauts rowed with all their strength. In the nick of time, they slipped past. The islands crashed together, just scraping the rear of the *Argo*. From that time on, the Symplegades have been no threat to sailors.

The sea held no further dangers, and the Argonauts sailed on. They passed the land of the Amazons, those warlike daughters of Ares, the god of war.[20] They also passed the great rock where the Titan Prometheus was chained, a vulture gobbling his liver.[21] Prometheus had been left there by Zeus in punishment for giving fire to man. The Argonauts didn't dare stop there.

The sailing was smooth, and the *Argo* soon reached Colchis. The brave fellows rejoiced as they touched shore. They believed the Golden Fleece was already theirs.

[19] (sim pleg' a dēz)

[20] (am'a zonz) (ar' ēz)

[21] (tī' tan)(prō mē' thūs or prō mē' thē us) The Titans were an early group of Greek gods. They lost the battle against Zeus when he attempted to become ruler of the heavens.

But the goddess Hera foresaw the dangers ahead. She had helped Jason this far. Now she was prepared to help him further. She knew that King Aeetes had a beautiful daughter, Medea.[22] Medea could perform all kinds of magic.

"Perfect," thought Hera. "Jason will need nothing less than the help of a **sorceress**. But how to make the girl fall in love with him?"

Hera sought out Aphrodite,[23] the goddess of love, for help. And Aphrodite in turn her son, Eros,[24] to cast a spell on poor Medea.

The young god of love agreed and hurried to Colchis with his bow and arrow.

The next day, the Argonauts made their way toward Aeetes' palace. They little knew how blessed they were. A mist, sent by Hera, hid them as they marched. It lifted to reveal them only when they were safely at the palace **threshold**. And Eros waited inside the palace for the perfect moment to strike Medea with love.

Jason was brought before Aeetes, who knew how to play the perfect host. Jason began to explain why he had come, but Aeetes interrupted.

"Please," he said. "Not a word until you've tasted of what my table offers. Then ask of me what you will." So a glorious feast was prepared.

Medea heard of the visitors' arrival. Curious, she quickly came to see them. But the minute she set eyes on Jason, Eros shot his arrow of love. He aimed well, and Medea's sad fate was sealed.

"What a handsome man that Jason is!" she whispered to herself. "The very sight of him burns into my heart!" She felt herself blush so deeply that she rushed away to her room. She couldn't let anyone know that she had fallen in love with a foreigner.

[22] (me dē' a)
[23] (af rō dī' tē)
[24] (er' os or ē' ros)

Soon the Argonauts had eaten well and felt totally re-freshed. "Now," asked Aeetes, "tell me what brings you to this corner of the world."

"We are adventurers from Greece," said Jason. "We've come for the Golden Fleece."

Aeetes frowned at this. Sensing the king's displeasure, Jason added, "We'll do anything you want in payment. We'll fight your wars, conquer your enemies, carry out any task. Just ask and it's yours."

Jason's offer meant nothing to Aeetes. "The nerve of these men!" he thought to himself. "They gobble up my food and drink. Then they demand the most precious thing I have! I should have killed them on sight!"

But Aeetes kept his anger to himself while planning his revenge. "Certainly, good fellow," he said to Jason with the falsest of smiles. "I'll give the Golden Fleece to you. But you must give me some sport in return. Perhaps enter-tain me with a show of bravery. What should it be?"

"The choice must be yours, Aeetes," said Jason.

Aeetes stopped to consider. Then he clapped his hands. "I've got it!" he said. "A simple task, and one I've done myself! I have two bulls with bronze hooves and iron-tipped horns. They're fierce-looking creatures and fire-breathers, too. But they'll be no match for you, I'm sure."

Aeetes smiled again. "Yoke these bulls together, Jason, and make them plow a field. Then take the teeth of the dragon that Cadmus[25] killed and plant them in the ground. They'll quickly grow into an army of warriors. You'll find them a little hot-tempered, too. You see, they'll be set on destroying you. But kill them all, and the Golden Fleece is yours."

Then Aeetes laughed cruelly. "It's a **trifle** that I ask, con-sidering the prize!" he declared. "So tell me, will you give it a try?"

Jason swallowed his fear. "What an old rascal!" he thought to himself. "I'm sure he never did such a thing in all his life. The question is—can I?"

[25] (kad′ mus) Cadmus was the legendary founder of the city of Thebes.

Nevertheless, Jason knew he had no choice. "I'll do this thing," he told Aeetes, "or die in the attempt."

Aeetes applauded him. "Tomorrow, then, good fellow, at the Grove of Ares! I'll look forward to it!"

Aeetes sat back, contented indeed. He felt confident Jason would die.

Jason and his crew returned to the ship. All that night they discussed Jason's **predicament**. Each of the Argonauts offered to perform the fearful task in Jason's place. But Jason would hear none of it.

In the middle of their debate, a young man appeared. He was Aeetes' grandson. Impressed by the brave heroes, he had come to offer his advice.

"My aunt Medea is your only hope," he told Jason. "She knows every kind of magic. Why, she can even stop the sun, moon, and stars dead in the sky. Surely she can give you magical power over mere bulls and warriors. I'll go and talk to her. Maybe I can persuade her to help you."

Deeply grateful, Jason urged the young man to hurry on his way. Of course, none of the Argonauts realized that Medea loved Jason. As they stood talking, she sat alone in her room weeping and cursing.

"Oh," she cried, "if my father knew that I loved a stranger! And an enemy! If he knew how tempted I am to go to Jason's aid! He'd wish me dead. And I deserved to be dead rather than think such **traitorous** thoughts."

Medea opened a box of poison, made from her own recipe. "Just a taste of these herbs," she said, "and I'll leave this world forever."

But she couldn't do it. She kept thinking of Jason, so brave and fine-looking. And she couldn't help but dream of being his wife, of having his children, of living with him happily forever. These thoughts, however impossible, made life too sweet to think of death.

She put the poison away and looked about for a different potion. "Ah, here it is," she said as she picked up another box. "An ointment made from the blood of Prometheus.

If Jason but puts it on his sword, he'll be safe from any danger. But how can I find him to give it to him?"

Her question was answered that very instant. Her nephew dashed into the room, begging her to go to Jason's aid. Barely able to contain her joy, Medea agreed.

"Go to Jason at once," she told her nephew. "Tell him to meet me within the hour."

"But where?" asked the nephew.

"Before the altar of Hecate,"[26] said Medea, "the goddess of darkness and magic."

Jason received Medea's message and hurried to the altar. Hera took care to make him still more charming, bathing him in golden light. When Medea arrived and saw him, she almost fainted. She was completely overwhelmed with love. She stared at him, **rapt** and silent.

Jason broke the silence. "Dear lady," he said, "I can only hope you are as merciful as you are beautiful. Do you have it in your power to help me? If so, I beg your aid."

Medea handed him the ointment. "Rub this on your sword," she said. "For one day only, it will make you **invincible**. And a day is all you need."

Jason held the small box in his hand uneasily. "Your ointment can't rid me of fear," he said. "Suppose too many soldiers sprout up from the dragon's teeth?"

"Then throw a rock at them!" said Medea with a laugh. "That will be enough, believe me!"

Jason laughed too, his fear completely gone. But proud Medea felt embarrassed as she looked at Jason. She knew she was hopelessly in love—and it showed! She turned away.

"Farewell," she said. "I must return to the palace. I ask nothing of you—except that you never forget me. Please, remember me with love, as I promise always to remember you."

But Jason pulled her back and led her to the altar.

"We'll have no talk of forgetfulness," said Jason. "You'll come back with me and be my bride. You'll be worshipped

---

[26] (hek' a tē)

and adored by all my people—but by none more than me. And only death will part us.''

At this, Medea was thrilled with hope and love. She went back to the palace overjoyed. Little did she realize that betrayal at Jason's hands awaited her. And little did Jason know his own hard fate. He should have been more careful of what he said before Hecate's altar, a place of such dark magic.

The next day, Jason went to the Grove of Ares. There Aeetes watched from his royal seat. Other Colchians were gathered on nearby hillsides.

Jason felt ready for Aeetes' test. His sword was already rubbed with ointment. Now he felt magical power rush through him.

The bulls were brought forth, stomping the ground and breathing fire. The grass shriveled and smoked beneath them. They sounded like roaring furnaces.

Jason's fear was **rekindled** for a moment. But as he approached the bulls, he saw no danger. He talked to the two beasts, petting and soothing them. Soon they were as mild as lambs. He was amazed at how easy it was to yoke them. And it took no trouble to make them plow the ground.

Aeetes frowned. "What magic is this?" he wondered. "Well, the dragon's teeth will put an end to Jason's trickery."

Aeetes handed the fearsome teeth to Jason, who scattered them on the ground. Fierce warriors sprouted up all around them. In no time at all, an entire army stood there.

Jason was taken aback. "Invincible or not," he thought, "I can't fight so many!"

But then he remembered Medea's words. He picked up a stone and threw it among the warriors.

At once the warriors forgot all about Jason and began to fight among themselves. They grabbed and stabbed and slashed one another. Within moments, the ground was covered with their bodies. Not one was left alive. And Jason hadn't struck a single blow.

The Argonauts raised a cheer, and Jason laughed with joy. But Aeetes found it no laughing matter. He stormed away to the palace.

"Trickery!" he roared. "Trickery and deceit! And I can see my daughter's hand in this. Yes, the traitorous girl has been bewitched by that thief Jason! Tomorrow at dawn, I'll send my army against the whole sneaking crew. I'll have every last one of them killed! My daughter, too, if she's among them! And I'll save Jason's skin for last!"

His wild shouts echoed through the palace halls. Medea heard his words and shivered with fear. She quickly sneaked out of the palace and found her way to the *Argo*. There she threw herself at Jason's knees and repeated her father's words.

"If you want the Golden Fleece, you must fetch it now," she urged. "You'll need my help against the dragon which protects it. But please, Jason, promise not to leave me at the mercy of my father."

Jason held her in his arms. "Have you forgotten my promises so quickly?" he asked her tenderly. "Didn't I swear to take you with me as my wife? Now come aboard, and show us the way to the Golden Fleece."

As night fell, they rowed swiftly up a river to the grove where the Golden Fleece was kept. Even in the twilight, the treasure shone brightly from its tree.

But there, too, was the dragon, ever alert and on guard. It was a fearsome sight with its lashing tongue and terrible fangs.

Jason reached for his sword, then stopped when Medea pulled him back. "I know a better way," she whispered.

Gently she crept toward the beast and sprinkled it with herbs. All the while, she sang lullabies in a soft voice.

"Poor, unsleeping creature," she cooed. "How long have you **craved** a little taste of sleep? Now is the time, now is the time. Sleep at last, tired dragon. Sleep."

The dragon's eyes closed. It toppled to the ground and rolled over on its back, snoring deeply.

At once Jason seized the Golden Fleece. Then he shouted to his crew, "Brave Argonauts! The Golden Fleece is ours! We'll rest till sunrise, when we can see our way past this rocky coast. Then we'll row like fury to the sea!"

But Medea knew that Jason faced certain defeat from Aeetes' army. She drew her nephew aside and said, "Go quickly to the palace. Tell my brother Apsyrtus[27] that I regret what I have done. Tell him I miss home and hate Jason but that I cannot escape. Ask him to come and rescue me at once. Add that I have the fleece and will surrender it on his arrival."

Her nephew did as he was told. By dawn, Apsyrtus had answered Medea's summons. He found all of Jason's crew were asleep. Only Medea remained awake, waiting for him.

"Father will be glad you've come to your senses," said Apsyrtus. "But where is the Golden Fleece? You promised its return."

Before he could speak another word, Medea struck him dead with her magic.

Dawn came and Jason and the Argonauts stirred. The shock of seeing Medea's dead brother stunned them into silence. Medea's grim face told them all they needed to know about the murder.

However, time was too short to wonder at the deed. After pausing to load Apsyrtus' body aboard the ship at Medea's order, they at once began rowing out to sea. Behind them came Aeetes' army in their own ships.

As fast as the *Argo* flew, Aeetes' fleet still gained. Jason tensely gripped his sword. "It's no good. We can't outrow them. We'll have to land and fight. Otherwise they'll burn the ship out from under us."

Medea standing at Jason's side shook her head. "Not so," she said, her eyes as cold as stone. "Just watch."

And in an instant, she hacked her brother's body to bits. One by one, she threw the pieces into the sea behind them.

Aeetes recognized his butchered son as the bloody limbs floated by. Wailing with grief, he slowed to gather the pieces

[27](ap sir' tus)

of Apsyrtus' body. That delay allowed the *Argo* to reach the sea. Otherwise, Jason and his crew would have been lost.

Jason watched Medea's deed with awe and terror. "What horrors might this woman do out of love for me?" he wondered. He would learn the answer one day, to his everlasting regret.

The return home was filled with danger. First, they came to a place dreaded by all sailors. It was the cliff of Scylla, where the whirlpool Charybdis[28] raged. That savage whirlpool swallowed everything which came near it. Gigantic waves crashed against the cliff, reaching up to the sky. But Hera saw the *Argo*'s danger and sent sea nymphs to guide the ship to safety.

After sailing for a long time, the Argonauts reached Crete.[29]

"And in good time," said Jason. "My men are thirsty and sea-weary. We can go to shore and rest."

"You cannot land," said Medea. "Talus lives here, the bronze giant made by Hephaestus.[30] Talus may be the last of his kind, but he shows no sign of wanting company. Believe me, your visit will be most unwelcome."

Jason was about to protest his disbelief. At that moment, Talus burst out of the sea with a terrible splash. He towered over the *Argo*, threatening to drop a huge boulder on the ship.

The Argonauts rowed furiously, trying to escape his reach. As they shouted and the giant roared, Medea prayed. "Blessed hounds of Hades,[31] hear me!" she cried. "This thing of metal can be hurt in just one spot. His heel is the place! Attack him there!"

Her prayer was answered. Talus was about to hurl his boulder when he struck his heel against a stone. He bled terribly and fainted away into the water, where he drowned.

---

[28] (sil' la) (ka rib' dis)
[29] (krēt)
[30] (tā' lus) (he fes' tus) Hephaestus was the god of metalworking.
[31] (hā' dēz) Hades was the Underworld region where most dead souls went. It was also the name of the ruler of the Underworld.

Jason's men let loose a wild cheer and rowed toward shore. There they enjoyed a welcome rest before sailing on.

When the *Argo* reached Thessaly, Jason proudly handed the fleece to Pelias.

"How can this be?" wondered Pelias. "I send the villain to his certain death. Yet here he is, safely returned! And now he'll want the kingdom as a reward. How shall I get rid of him?"

But outwardly, Pelias was all smiles and gladness. "We must celebrate your return Jason," he declared. "So let's feast for a month. And to end the feast in grand style, you shall be crowned."

Jason was satisfied and accepted Pelias' promise. Yet to him, the celebration seemed strangely incomplete. At last he realized what was wrong.

He turned to a servant and said, "My father! I haven't seen him since I came home. Why isn't he here to celebrate his son's return?"

"Aeson?" said the man. "Alas, he's old and ailing. No one expects him to live for long."

The news saddened Jason. Turning to Medea, he said, "This glorious day seems empty without my father here. Can your magic help him? I'll gladly give up a few years of my own life to lengthen his."

Medea smiled. "A generous offer, my love," she replied. "But I can restore your father at no cost to your own life."

On the next full moon, Medea went out into the night alone. She sang magical **incantations** to the stars, the moon, and Hecate. As she chanted, the stars actually seemed to brighten.

Suddenly a gleaming chariot pulled by dragons dropped from the sky. Medea stepped in the chariot and flew into the heavens.

For days and nights, Medea searched for the magic roots and herbs she needed. She never slept, ate, or spoke to a soul in all that time. Jason's happiness was all she thought of. Finally on the ninth night, she found the last herb for her spell and headed home.

When Medea returned, she asked that Aeson be brought forth. The poor man was on the brink of death and had to be carried to her. Medea placed him on a bed of herbs and lulled him to sleep.

"You must leave us now," said Medea to Jason and his men. "No one must observe the ceremony by which I restore Aeson's youth."

Once she was alone, Medea stirred up a boiling brew of her mix. Next, she cut Aeson's throat and drained his body of blood. Then she filled his veins with the potion.

No sooner had Medea completed her magic than Aeson's gray hair turned black. Wrinkles of forty years vanished. His muscles grew strong again.

Soon Aeson stirred from his magic sleep. He sat up, astonished at his new **vitality**. He happily rejoined Jason, who felt that now his joy was complete.

But Medea sensed that all was not well. She looked into King Pelias' eyes and saw evil thoughts.

"He'll take my beloved's life," she thought. "Unless I take his first."

After turning over many plans, Medea grimly decided what she must do. At once she carried out her scheme by going to Pelias' daughters.

"I've seen how much you love your father," the sorceress said. "How sad you must be that he is old and soon to die! Surely you've heard what I did for Aeson. I can restore your father's youth as well."

"But no one witnessed what magic you worked on Aeson," said one daughter. "Give us a demonstration so we can believe your words."

Clever Medea agreed. Before the girls' eyes, she took an old ram and cut him limb from limb. Then she put the pieces in a huge pot and spoke a magic spell. At once a lamb leapt out of the pot, full of youth and energy.

"In this way I can restore your father's youth—if you will help," Medea said.

The girls agreed, hardly able to contain their joy. They wanted to go to their father and tell him their plan. But Medea swore them to secrecy. She pointed out that Pelias might be uneasy about relying on magic.

That night, she gave Pelias a sleeping potion.

"Now, girls," she said. "You must cut your father up, as I did the ram."

The poor girls could barely force themselves to carry out the deed. But Medea reminded them of the happy change in store.

After butchering their father, the daughters put his bloody limbs into the huge pot. Then they waited for Medea to utter her spell. But Medea was gone. Pelias' daughters wept and wailed, realizing they had killed their father.

In the end, Medea's evil deed did Jason little good. Because of Pelias' murder, she and Jason were forced to flee the kingdom. They decide to journey to Corinth, where Creon was king.[32] There they lived happily for ten years and had two sons.

Sometimes during those years, Medea thought longingly of home. But she knew she could never return to her father. Besides, the people of Corinth treated her well, and she loved Jason dearly.

However, a bitter day came for Medea. Jason decided to abandon her and marry Creon's daughter, Creusa.[33] Jason felt no real love for the girl. But it seemed a wise idea to marry her. He would gain great power and wealth by doing so.

Jason didn't dare tell Medea about the plan. But the news soon reached her anyway. When she heard, she flew into a rage. "I'll not let it happen!" she cried. "The girl will die before she marries Jason!"

Reports of Medea's rage reached King Creon, who feared for his daughter. Creon acted quickly. He sent word to

[32] (kor' inth) (krē' on)
[33] (krē ū' sa)

Medea that she and her children must go into **exile**.

While Medea wept, Jason came to her with unkind words.

"A fine fool you've been," he said. "That threat you made almost got you killed. I had to persuade Creon to sentence you to exile, not death. It wasn't easy, given your threats. You have me to thank for your life."

"Thank you?" exclaimed Medea. "What kind of life will my children and I have? Do you know what exile will be like for us?"

"I'll give you gold to help you on your way," said Jason.

"But have you forgotten what you owe me? Have you forgotten how I killed to save your life?"

"Why should I be grateful to you?" Jason angrily replied. "I can thank Hera, Aphrodite, and Eros. It's to them I owe my success, not you."

Medea screamed in rage at these cruel words. "What spell have I been under?" she cried. "I've been tricked by the gods into loving an unloving man. Get out of my sight!"

Jason left, and Medea at once plotted her revenge. "I must appear to make peace with Creusa," she thought. "I'll give her a gift—one that suits her **vanity**."

So Medea found a beautiful gown and sprinkled it with terrible poison. She then wrapped the dress in a cloth and gave it to her sons.

"Go," she told them. "Take this to Creusa. Tell her it's a gift from me. Tell her that I seek forgiveness and wish her happiness."

The boys carried out their mother's orders. Creusa, in her vanity, couldn't resist putting on the gown at once. As soon as the cloth touched her skin, she was swallowed up by fire. Though she tried to rip away the gown, it clung to her. Her flesh burned away, and she died in great pain.

With horror, Medea realized what her next deed must be.

"What becomes of me no longer matters," she said. "Death would be most welcome. But my beloved sons . . . . I can't let them suffer for what I've done."

So, with a parting kiss, she cut the throats of her two boys. Medea made sure they died less painfully than Creusa.

Jason, who had heard of Medea's plans from a servant, rushed to the scene. But he was too late. He arrived to see Medea flying away in a chariot pulled by dragons. No words of hate—or even love—could bring her back. Already this part of her life was as dead as her two young sons.

Medea eventually fled to Athens.[34] She lived there for a time as the wife of King Aegeus.[35] But her life was always troubled, ruined by her love for Jason.

And what became of the Golden Fleece? Some say that Jason placed it inside a temple of Zeus. If so, it has long since vanished from the spot. Even the gods don't know its whereabouts. Certainly it brought no happiness to Jason.

And Jason? Without adventure and love, his life had no meaning. He wandered through Greece, lonely and friendless. One day, Jason sat beside the *Argo*, sadly remembering his past. The front of the rotting ship fell and killed him instantly.

It was not an end that Jason would have liked. Surely he would have preferred to die facing danger. But perhaps it was fitting that he end his life alone and unloved.

[34](ath′ enz)
[35](ē′ jus or ē′ jē us)

INSIGHTS

According to one myth, a Boy Scout deed helped Jason win the Golden Fleece. On his way to first claim the throne from Pelias, Jason stopped at a river. There he found an old woman who was too frail to cross. Jason picked her up and took her to the other side. As he climbed up the muddy bank, he lost one sandal. (Which explains how the prophecy came true.)

That old woman turned out to be Hera in disguise. Jason's kind action explains why the goddess always helped him afterwards.

The root *naut* comes from Latin and Greek words meaning *sailor* or *ship*. Today the root can still be seen in words such as *nautical* (referring to shipping) and *nautilus* (a spiral-shelled ocean creature). And in the spirit of the adventurer Jason, we speak of space explorers as *astronauts* and *cosmonauts*.

Medea's trail of evil doesn't end with this story. She later married the king of Athens. However, she lost this husband, too. When the king discovered Medea had tried to poison his son, Theseus, he ordered her to leave. Medea then finally returned to her father in Colchis.

The most familiar stories of the *Argo*'s voyage center on Medea. But she wasn't even in earlier versions. Instead, the emphasis was on the famous heroes who sailed with Jason. After all, they were quite a collection. Perhaps only the Trojan War involved more great men.

continued

That is why the list of those who sailed on the *Argo* tended to change over time. Later retellers of the myth listed among the crew ancestors of people they knew. Saying that someone's great-great-grandfather had been an Argonaut was fine flattery indeed.

The golden ram in this myth should be familiar to all students of astrology and astronomy. After the ram was sacrificed to Zeus, it became part of the zodiac as the constellation Aries. *Aries* is the Latin word for *ram*.

Since the myth of Jason was first told, *fleece* has taken on some different meanings. Now one definition of the word is "to cheat or rob by trickery." It's that meaning Senator William Proxmire had in mind. He created the Golden Fleece Award, which he gave out every year. This award went to the government project Proxmire considered the biggest waste of funds. Not quite the prize Jason would want!

GODS AND HEROES OF GREEK AND ROMAN MYTHOLOGY

Greek Name	Roman Name
Aphrodite	Venus
(Phoebus) Apollo	(Phoebus) Apollo
Ares	Mars, Mavors
Artemis	Diana
(Pallas) Athena	Minerva
Cronus	Saturn
Demeter	Ceres
Dionysus, Bacchus	Bacchus, Liber
Eros	Cupid
Gaea	Ge, Earth, Terra
Hades, Pluto	Pluto, Dis
Helios, Hyperion	Sol
Hephaestus	Vulcan, Mulciber
Hera	Juno
Heracles	Hercules
Hermes	Mercury
Hestia	Vesta
Odysseus	Ulysses
Persephone, Kore	Proserpina, Proserpine
Poseidon	Neptune
Rhea	Ops
Uranus	Uranus, Coelus
Zeus	Jupiter, Jove